WEBB QUARTERHILL

had fought with honor for the South.
He had enlisted as a buck private
in the U.S. Indian Fighting Army—
and the first man he met at Fort
McKeogh was Major Mark Faro—
the man he had held as a prisoner
during the Civil War, the man who
would do his best to kill Quarterhill because the ex-Johnny Reb knew
things that could break the Major.

*   *   *

Now, because of a crazy set of circumstances, they were involved in an
action together. And all the Major
needed was a back to shoot at.

Also by William Chamberlain

THE TRUMPETS OF COMPANY K

This is an original publication—not a reprint.

FORCED MARCH
TO LOON CREEK

William Chamberlain

BALLANTINE BOOKS   NEW YORK

SBN 345-02601-2-075

First Printing: October, 1964
Second Printing: May, 1972

Printed in the United States of America

BALLANTINE BOOKS, INC.
101 Fifth Avenue, New York, N.Y. 10003
An Intext Publisher

Fort McKeogh, Wyoming Territory

The train was the only sign of life in this dun land as it hustled along through the hot afternoon, screened by its plume of black smoke. Ahead of it, the rails ran away toward hazy mountains vaguely shaped in the heat shimmer; on either side was the vast reach of empty distances. This was Sioux country, and an uneasy truce still held it in this summer of 1872—a ragged truce that was already fraying toward the edge of war.

Wyoming Territory.

Inside the coach, only partly filled, the air hung in a heavy, noxious cloud unrelieved by any freshness, for the windows were shut tight against the smoke and cinders spewed by the laboring engine. The passengers rode in stoic discomfort, clothes sticking to their bodies as they mopped at the sweat that ran down their faces. They were of all kinds and of many callings: unshaven men wearing range clothes; travelers from the east, their paper collars wilted into soggy messes; a preacher dressed in sober black; a gambler garbed much the same way.

One woman rode at the far end of the car, set a little apart from the rest. She alone, of all of them, seemed not to be distressed by the hot, grimy air or the sweltering discomfort of the rocking coach. She looked out of the smeared window at the dun landscape as it flew by, wrapped in some inner aloofness of her own that ignored the rudeness of her surroundings.

Webb Quarterhill, balancing himself against the jerky sway of the train, dipped water out of the keg fastened at the end of the coach and studied her profile as he drank from the tin cup. She had gotten on at Julesburg earlier in the day, and off and on as he had ridden with the baker's dozen of recruits from Jefferson Barracks at the far end of the coach, he had speculated idly as to who she was. Not that he really cared, or that he would ever likely see her again, he decided.

She was in her early twenties, he thought, perhaps twenty-four—seven years younger than he. Not exactly beautiful, but attractive. She had an oval face, composed and thoughtful, which was framed by dark hair. Her eyes were dark too, he saw as she turned her head and her eyes met his for a brief moment. On a sudden impulse, Quarterhill rinsed the cup and refilled it, and moved easily along the aisle to stop beside her seat.

"It's lukewarm and it tastes pretty much of alkali, ma'am," he said. "But it's wet. Would you care . . ."

He stood there, a faint smile erasing the harder lines of his face as he looked down at her. He was a tall man, rangily built, with wide shoulders and the slim hips of a horseman. Four years of war had left their mark on him—a touch of gray in his black hair at the temples, a little sadness about his features when they were in repose.

For a moment the girl didn't answer as she looked up at him, her eyes a little startled. She took in the stiff newness of the recruit's uniform that had been issued to him at Jefferson Barracks—the cavalry uniform with blue blouse and breeches of lighter blue, striped with yellow at the seams, yellow kerchief tied loosely at the throat. Lee Howell knew the uniform; she had grown up in the cavalry.

A recruit's uniform, she thought. *Yet he is no recruit. He has worn the uniform somewhere before.*

"Thank you," she said gravely, taking the cup that he held down to her. "You are very kind."

He waited while she drank slowly, his eyes leaving her alone as he looked at the pattern of the country sliding by beyond the smeared window. He was aware that she was holding the empty cup out to him, and he inclined his head briefly as he took it.

"Thank you," she said again, her mouth making a faintly wry grimace. "As you said, it is wet."

Quarterhill stood there for a moment longer, looking down at her. Then he murmured, "You are quite welcome," and went back to put the tin cup on its shelf above the water

6

keg. As he returned along the aisle he was aware that the faces of his fellow recruits—and that of Corporal Clem Clendenning, who was convoying them from Jefferson Barracks to Fort McKeogh—were watching him with varying expressions. Clendenning's lips twisted unpleasantly.

"Flyin' pretty high for a lousy recruit, ain't you?" he said heavily. "If you're lookin' to cut yourself a piece of *that* cake, you can damn well forget it, see?"

"So?" Quarterhill said, his voice betraying nothing.

He stood for a moment, his body swaying to the jerky motion of the train as his eyes wandered indifferently over the faces looking up at him. They were faces that meant little to him, other than that they belonged to men who were bound for the same regiment that he was. He knew none of them well; he would accept them for what time proved them to be.

Clendenning slouched his big, untidy body deeper into the seat. The leer became broader on his heavy mouth. "Yeah, so," he said, his voice suddenly angry. "That dame has got 'officer's woman' written all over her, recruit. She ain't for your kind; you'll find that out soon enough once we get to McKeogh. Not that she's any better than the rest!"

Quarterhill pulled his attention back to the big corporal—didn't like what he saw. Clendenning was a heavily built man, his face blotched and red from countless bouts with the bottle. Webb had learned to detest him during the trip from Jefferson Barracks. The man was a braggart and a bully possessed of a vile and poisonous tongue, which he had used lavishly on the men in his charge. He was also a coward. Quarterhill had found that out before the detachment had ever left Jefferson Barracks.

Clendenning had mistaken Quarterhill's quietness for timidity and had ridden him with rough spurs at the barracks. One night he had given Quarterhill a particularly virulent tongue lashing over a trifling matter, and Quarterhill had invited the corporal to step out with him behind the stables, where the matter could be settled. Although Clendenning had a good inch in height and forty pounds in weight over Quarterhill, he had backed weakly down. But the matter had not ended there, Quarterhill knew.

He said thinly now, "Suppose we just leave it at that,

corporal. Who the lady is or what she is is none of your business—or mine."

The spite deepened in Clendenning's eyes. "Seems to me you're actin' pretty high and mighty over some goddamn' tart just because you give her a drink of——"

"I said leave it alone," Quarterhill interrupted, his voice suddenly hard. "Either keep your filthy mouth off her, or I'll fill it full of teeth for you!"

He saw the wicked vindictiveness that came into the corporal's eyes for a moment, but Clendenning passed the matter off with a shrug. "Aw, what the hell," he grunted. "If you want it that way, you can have it. Set down!"

Quarterhill stood there a moment longer, indifferent to the stares of the others: the Swede Larsen, with his forelock of tow hair falling down into his eyes; the small man named Tash, who watched with a sly interest in his sharp, weasel-like face; Mulroney, the ex-pugilist, with his pale eyes staring unblinkingly from beneath the scar tissue that marked his heavy brows. Then Quarterhill moved with deliberation past Clendenning to drop into his seat.

The incident wasn't closed, Quarterhill knew. He had backed Clendenning down in front of the other recruits and the man would not forgive that. Well, he'd worry about it when he had to.

He turned his attention to the grimy window beside him, getting a smudged view of the country outside as it ran toward him. The grade had now entered a canyon, to follow the course of the river that alternately raced, white-maned, through gorges choked with boulders, and meandered lazily across flats covered with alder and birch and cottonwood. It was pretty country, Quarterhill knew, a fresh and unsoiled country vastly different from that he had left behind. Against his will, his thoughts went back to the pine uplands of Georgia where he had been born.

But he did not remember it as it had been when he was a kid playing about the acres of Fair Oaks, his father's plantation. He remembered it as it had been when he returned there after the surrender at Appomattox. That had not been a pleasant return. In his mind he could still see the blackened chimneys, standing like sad monuments above the ruins of what had once been houses. He could remember

8

the desolation of Atlanta and the waste of once-prosperous fields now claimed by nothing but weeds.

There had been little left of Fair Oaks beyond charred timbers, overgrown with vines, and stables and outbuildings falling down. He had not stayed, for there was nothing to keep him. His father was dead in a northern prison; his only brother had been killed in Longstreet's bloody battle that second day at Gettysburg. Mary Sue Carver, the girl he had meant to marry, had died of the typhoid in the third year of the war.

So he had drifted and the years had gone by. Texas and Mexico: he had found little there that interested him. He had turned northward; the grimy bustle of mushrooming cities had increased his unrest. In St. Louis the solution to the thing he was seeking finally came to him.

A simple solution. At Jefferson Barracks he had raised his hand and taken the oath, and he was in the Army again—even though it was an army that wore the uniform against which he had fought for four years. It had not been too difficult a thing to do, for he still wore the mark of West Point within him, despite the fact that he had left the stern gray school on the Hudson to fight for the South more than ten years ago.

Soldiering was the only thing he knew, and he felt at home in uniform, even though it was a recruit's ill-fitting clothes . . . and even though he had traded for a private's low estate the captain's insignia that he had once worn. He was not sorry; he faced the future with equanimity. . . .

Quarterhill pulled himself abruptly back to the present. The canyon floor had broadened into flats covered with sagebrush and flanked by low foothills spotted with pine and fir. The day was wearing into late afternoon. The faint hoot of the engine whistle drifted back along the side of the train, and the wheels, clacking over the rail joints, took on a different sound as they began to slow. The conductor came through the car.

"Sunbeam," he was saying. "Sunbeam in five minutes." He added as he came abreast of the group of recruits, "Yore stop for Fort McKeogh, corporal. Guess you know that."

"I know it well enough," Clendenning said sourly. "All right, you birds. Get your goddamn' gear."

9

The first signs of the town began to slide by the windows: corrals and sheds and a few unpainted buildings, weathered gray by the sun. Now more solid buildings came along, but they too were marked by the rawness of this new land. The train was moving slowly now, and Quarterhill got to his feet and fumbled in the rack for the small bag that held shaving gear and other toilet articles, plus the few personal trinkets which were all that linked him with the life that he had turned his back upon.

"Shake it up," Clendenning growled. "We ain't got all day. I hope to God they got an ambulance waitin' for us."

"How far to the fort, corporal?" someone asked.

"Four mile . . . and if there's no ambulance, you hoof it."

"Christ, I ain't no damn' doughboy. I joined up with the Army to ride."

Soldier talk that means nothing, Quarterhill thought. *Still, it is a good thing to hear again.*

The train came to a jarring stop, and Clendenning herded his recruits onto the wooden platform that ran a way beside the tracks. There was a one-room depot, and beyond was the dusty main street with its assorted traffic: a freight wagon, loaded high and pulled by six horses, creaking along through the dust; a pair of riders jogging toward the road that stretched across the flats beyond; false-front buildings with covered stoops and board sidewalks running in front of them; horses standing at the hitch rails in front of the general store and the three saloons.

It was good. Quarterhill liked it as he stood a little apart from the others while he took it in. The sun was dropping toward the mountains to the west and the slanting rays of the light endowed the town with a grace that it would not otherwise possess.

"Stay here while I see what's what," Clendenning was saying. "You're in charge, Tash."

The corporal moved across the platform and disappeared among the sheds at the rear of the depot. Quarterhill sucked in air that was fresh with the smell of sage and pine, and he had the satisfying feeling that at last he had come home—home to a land and a fort that he had never seen, but home just the same. He felt alive for the first time in a long while.

That feeling of well-being was rudely shattered. He was standing midway along the coach when an officer, wearing highly polished boots and a major's insignia, stepped from the train to the platform. His back was toward Quarterhill as he turned to reach up a helping hand to the girl whom Quarterhill had spoken with briefly inside the coach earlier. Now he assisted her onto the platform, and a trooper followed, carrying bags.

The major's voice carried to Quarterhill. "By Gad, Miss Howell—Lee," he was saying, "renewing our acquaintance out here in this blasted country is a rare stroke of luck."

Quarterhill scowled blackly. He had heard that voice somewhere before, he knew. He had the feeling that it hadn't been under pleasant circumstances. The major had turned to the soldier now, and his voice became sharper and more domineering.

"Don't just stand there, man! Go and bring the ambulance! Move lively, confound you! Do you expect Miss Howell to walk through this dust?"

So her name is Lee Howell, Quarterhill thought.

It was an absent thought, for his attention was on the major, whose back was still toward him. Lee Howell had turned a little, and when she saw Quarterhill standing by the coach, she gave him a small nod with a hint of friendliness in it. The major turned now, so that Quarterhill could see his face. With effort Quarterhill kept his own face impassive, controlling the shock that ran through him as he looked back at the other.

My God, he thought. *It can't be . . . but it is! I couldn't forget that face! Even after eight years!*

It was a face that was a little fuller now—a little more flushed by good living. But it still had the chiseled features and the handsome arrogance that it had possessed on that night when Webb Quarterhill had first seen it in the valley of the Shenandoah. It had belonged to Brevet Lieutenant Colonel Mark Faro, United States Army, then. In the second that he stood staring, memory of that night flashed through Quarterhill's mind.

Just at twilight, there had been a wild and savage fight

11

at a crossroads named Bailey's Corners. Quarterhill's hard-pressed troop had been a part of Jubal Early's rear guard after Early's defeat at Winchester that same day. Just as dark was coming down, Quarterhill's ragged troopers had brought in half a dozen Union prisoners, among them Brevet Lieutenant Colonel Mark Faro. Quarterhill, knowing the long, hard march that lay ahead of them that night, could not be hampered by prisoners.

He had accepted Faro's parole—his word of honor—that, if released, he and the men with him would take no further part in the war, and that they would not divulge information of what they had seen that night which might be hurtful to the desperate Confederate cause. With Mark Faro's promise, his solemn word as an officer, Quarterhill had let them go.

It was not until the war was long over that he had learned that Faro had violated that parole—that the information he had carried back to the Union lines that night had contributed heavily to Early's disastrous defeat at Fisher's Hill three days later. Quarterhill had learned other things as well. Faro had not told his superiors of his parole; he had claimed, instead, that he had escaped from the Confederates at great personal risk in order to carry vital information back. Another brevet promotion had been Mark Faro's reward for that infamous lie.

And now he was here at Fort McKeogh!

Hot anger shook Quarterhill in that split second as he stood there with the bitter memory running through his mind. He thought savagely: *If I had a sidearm I'd shoot the bastard down where he stands!* With an effort he got his anger under control. It was no good, he knew. He was wearing a different uniform now. He was an enlisted man and Faro was an officer; all of the cards would be stacked against the recruit.

With icy control he forced himself to square his shoulders and turn out the salute that was called for; with hard satisfaction he saw the startled look that came into Faro's eyes as he returned the salute and recognized Quarterhill. *Damn his soul,* Quarterhill thought coldly. *Now let him sweat!* And sweat he would, he knew, because Mark Faro could not afford to have it known throughout the Army that he was a liar and a man without honor—an officer who had broken his sacred parole. He would be through—personally, if not officially.

Quarterhill half expected that Faro would move toward him—brace him here and now—but the major dropped his hand and turned away. That would not be the end of it, Quarterhill knew. Faro would try to destroy him; the man had no other choice. How he would go about it was something that Quarterhill couldn't guess now. He'd take care of it when the time came, he decided indifferently.

He heard Faro's voice lifted petulantly as he spoke to Lee Howell. "You know that man, Miss Howell?" he asked. "I thought that I saw you nod."

"He very kindly brought me a drink of water on the train," Lee Howell answered.

The petulance deepened in Faro's voice. "You have been reared in the Army, Lee—Miss Howell," he said. "You should know better than to encourage an enlisted man. Especially the sort that we are getting these days. They are cattle."

"I was not encouraging him, major," Lee said, a little coolness coming into her voice. "About courtesy I'll make my own decisions. Here comes the ambulance."

Quarterhill turned away. Corporal Clendenning was coming back down the platform, a heavy-set trooper walking beside him. The stranger's seamed face bore the marks of countless barroom brawls and there was a quizzical good humor in his blue eyes as he cocked an inquiring eyebrow at the group of recruits. Quarterhill noted that patches, less sun-faded than the rest of the cloth, showed where sergeant's stripes had once been on the man's sleeves. He and Clendenning halted in front of the others.

"So them's our new heroes," the ex-sergeant said to Clendenning. "I must of seen worse, but I don't remember where. What'd you do—empty the St. Louis gutters, corporal?"

"I took what they give me," Clendenning said sourly. "An' I'll thank you to keep a civil tongue in your head, now that you're no longer wearin' the stripes, Garbish."

"Well, now, I'll try to remember," Garbish said, unbothered. "Come on, buckoes. We'll load up, although I do not count it a kindly thing that Mitch Garbish—once sergeant—should be torn away from McCarthy's Saloon just to haul

13

such an unpromisin' bunch as you look to be out to Fort McKeogh."

He led the way and the rest followed him through the dust and behind a shed back of the depot, where an Army ambulance and a hitched team waited. The recruits crowded into the light vehicle, sitting on seats that ran along the sides, knees bumping as they faced each other. Garbish and Clendenning climbed onto the seat in front and Garbish took the reins.

The ambulance moved off, skirted the shed, and turned into the town's main street. It was close to sunset now, and the slanting rays of the sun lent a little softness to the fronts of the unpainted buildings. People moved along the board sidewalks—women holding their skirts and with shawls or bonnets or chip hats on their heads; swaggering range riders, their spurs jingling; staid townsmen, dressed in sober and nondescript garb. Here and there a blanketed reservation Indian stood back from the traffic as he stared ahead from an impassive and sullen face.

There was a livery stable with doors opening to the gloom behind. A barber shop advertised *Bath—Four Bits*. A hotel, more pretentious than the rest, had two stories and a balcony with a railing around it. Near the end of the street a square, ugly building wore a sign, *McCarthy's Sundance Saloon*, painted on its false front. Garbish turned his head to squint at it and blow his breath out gustily as the ambulance passed.

"It is a hell of a note for a man to leave a town while he is still thirsty," he complained, then shrugged. "Aw, well, I've drunk up all of the money I had anyway."

They came to the edge of the town, and he put the team into a trot. The road, straight as a string, was deep in dust that drifted up, embracing the ambulance and its passengers as the wheels churned it. Quarterhill, sitting just behind the driver's seat, twisted so that he could see past Garbish's bulk in front of him. The fort was ahead in the red eye of the sinking sun; they would reach it at about time for Retreat, he guessed.

Well ahead of them was another ambulance, a mounted man riding alongside. Lee Howell and Mark Faro, he

14

thought. That guess was confirmed by Mitch Garbish a moment later.

"Major Faro and Colonel Howell's daughter up ahead," he grunted. "She's been visitin' in the East. On her way now to join the colonel over at the Galena Indian Agency, so I hear."

"Now that's interesting," Clendenning said with elaborate sarcasm. "And how come *you* know so much about it?"

"There ain't much that the barracks don't hear," Garbish told him complacently. "I keep my ears open."

"Is Faro that snotty-lookin' major I seen at the depot?" Corporal Clendenning asked sourly. "He must be new—I ain't seen him around here before that I recall."

Garbish spat into the dust. "He ain't none of ourn," he said. "He come out here from Washington to inspect the regiment. Regiment was already gone."

"Gone where?"

"How the hell would I know?" Garbish asked amiably. "I was in the guardhouse when they left. I hear it, though, that General Gilmorin has got bit by the glory bug again—claims that the Sioux is about to bust out of the reservations in force. Anyhow, the regiment has gone to join him on the Powder."

"The whole regiment gone?"

"Yep. Except for them degenerate characters which was in the guardhouse and the halt and the lame in the hospital and a few other odds and ends," Garbish agreed. "Includin' the Old Man, whose rheumatism was kickin' up too bad for him to set in a saddle. He's settin' at home, swearin' a blue streak, instead."

"You mean Colonel Bexar?"

"Who the hell else would I mean?"

"I guess I timed my gettin' back to McKeogh just right," Clendenning said smugly. "I ain't lost nothing on the Powder and that damn' fool Gilmorin can hunt his damn' Injuns without no help from me. I don't crave no glory."

"That ain't no way to talk," Garbish said virtuously. "Think of all them innocent recruits back there. Don't you want 'em to think you're a hero?"

"Horse manure," Clendenning grunted. "I don't care what they think of me."

The evening gun sounded, putting its *boom* into the sunset when they were still half a mile from the fort. Across the distance, Quarterhill could see the flag coming down—could hear the faint echoes of a trumpet sounding "To the Colors." It put a good feeling into him all at once. He was coming home.

2

The Fight in the Sutler's Store

First Lieutenant Jacob Miller, Officer of the Day, made his customary rounds of barracks and stables after taking Retreat. He, with the lieutenant commanding the infantry detachment and the incapacitated Colonel Bexar, were the only line officers left here.

Miller was a slender, graying man of middle height with a thoughtful face burned dark by wind and sun. He had spent almost twenty years out here on the frontier, and promotion had passed him by. He had resigned himself to that—expected no more than that he should finish his service out here where he had begun it. Such things were, and you could not change them; nor would they change by themselves, so he had thought.

But he had been wrong. He still found it hard to believe. Ten days ago, just before the regiment had left for the Powder, orders had come from Washington assigning him to duty at West Point—something that he had often dreamed about but had never really thought would come true. Three days hence he would take the train for the East. . . .

He went into the single room of his Spartan quarters, hung up saber and pistol belt, and stripped to the waist. In the lean-to at the rear of the quarters he washed off the dirt of the day, went back into the room buttoning his shirt—to find Sergeant Major Ed Harvey at the open door waiting for him.

"Well, sergeant," Miller asked in his pleasant, unassuming voice, "anything that I can do for you?"

Ed Harvey came in, turning out his careful salute with the ease of long practice. He was a craggy-faced man with frosty blue eyes, and the marks of his long service lay deep on him. In a way, he and Jacob Miller were friends.

"I have to report, sir," he said in his gravelly voice, "that Major Faro has returned from Sunbeam bringin' Colonel Howell's daughter with him. He has took her to the colonel's quarters, where she will stay the night with Colonel Bexar an' his lady. Does the lootenant know if she will be goin' on by stage to Galena Agency tomorrow? It comes to me that she should have an escort—though where we would get one, I do not know."

Miller fastened the last button of his shirt and stuffed the tail of it into his breeches. "I will speak with the colonel about the matter, sergeant," he said. "I take it that the recruit contingent from Jefferson Barracks came on the same train?"

"They did, sir, and a sorry bunch that they are," Harvey said dourly. "Half of 'em lookin' over their shoulder for the sheriff, I would be willing to bet."

"Where'd you put them?"

"In D Troop's barracks, with Clendenning in charge. They are eatin' now. After supper they will draw equipment. Tomorrow I will have them out early tryin' to make soldiers of them—although I misdoubt that God himself could do that."

Miller smiled faintly. "They'll come along, Ed," he said. "None among them with former service, I take it?"

"None that will admit it," Harvey grunted. "There is one—a man by the name of Quarterhill—that has seen service, though, or I miss my guess. I will speak with him tomorrow."

"Quarterhill . . ." Miller murmured. "An unusual name. I have heard it before, I think. Where I do not know."

After Harvey had gone, Miller mixed himself a thin drink and took it and his cigar out to the rawhide chair on the tiny verandah, where he could catch a hint of the breeze that came with sundown. He sat down and crossed his knees as he stared across the baked parade ground. The orderly row of barracks was over there, each with its cookhouse behind. Farther back was the line of stables. To his right, closing the end of the parade, was the headquarters building, the flagpole out in front with the saluting cannon flanking it. Along his own line were the other officers' quarters, Colonel Bexar's set at the end.

He would miss all of this, Miller supposed; after all, it had been a part of his life for so long. He was a lonely man who had never married, for opportunity had never offered. That might be changed, he supposed, when he was at West Point.

He savored the fragrance of his cigar and had a small sip of his whiskey as he allowed his mind to wander back to that gray school on the Hudson. *Has it changed much?* he wondered. There were ways, of course, in which it would never change. The green plain above the river, surrounded by its stately trees, would still be there; the stern pile of the cadet barracks would be the same. Storm King would not have changed. The river would still sweep majestically out of the highlands, and old Fort Putnam would still look solidly down from the hills.

Jacob Miller was not a sentimental man, but the thought of going home put a swift elation in him now. He'd be going home in more ways than one, for he'd been born in a little house just off the post where his mother still lived. She'd be sixty-seven, he remembered absently. Time certainly got away from a man; it was close to ten years since he'd last seen her.

He wondered how she'd look. About the same as she always had, he guessed; at any rate, her letters hadn't changed. They came once a month, as regular as clockwork, and they were as filled with chatty gossip about the Point as they had always been. His mother had seen a lot of classes come and go from that austere academy porched above the river; she was a woman who took an interest in such things. . . .

Colonel Bexar's orderly marched along the walk to halt in front of Miller and turn out a smart salute. "Colonel's compliments, lootenant," he said, running his words together. "He says would the lootenant join him and his lady for supper, sir? Major Faro an' Miss Howell will be there."

A faint flush of pleasure showed briefly in Jacob Miller's sunburned face. The invitation was a welcome one; it would be a pleasant contrast to the lonely supper that he had been contemplating at the deserted mess.

"My compliments to Colonel Bexar, Haynes," he said. "Say to him that I accept with pleasure."

Major Mark Faro, stripped to the waist in the stuffy heat that still filled his room at the Bachelor Officers' Quarters, got a fresh bottle of whiskey from the specially fitted cowhide bag in the closet, and carefully locked the closet door again. He carried the bottle to the table in the center of the room and worried the cork out with fingers that shook a little. The neck of the bottle beat a little tattoo against the rim of the tumbler as he splashed a generous portion of liquor into the glass.

He needed this drink—needed it damned bad, he was thinking as he raised the glass to his lips. Seeing Quarterhill back there on that depot platform had given him a nasty few moments an hour ago. No doubt but that the man had recognized him; he had seen that wicked recognition in the other's eyes.

He took half the drink down in a long swallow, gagging and shuddering a little as the fiery stuff bit at his throat. Then that welcome, familiar warmth began to grow in his belly, and he felt confidence returning to him as he carried bottle and glass across the room and sat in a worn leather chair.

His thoughts became more orderly now as he stretched out his legs and relaxed. All right, suppose the man to whom he had given his parole *was* a soldier here in this regiment? Even if Quarterhill was inclined to make a formal charge, what the hell good would it do? It would be a recruit's word against that of a commissioned officer, wouldn't it? An officer with influence in Washington. Even old Bexar would think twice before he gave any credence to any accusation Quarterhill might make.

Faro took down the rest of his drink and again was conscious of that welcome warmth within him. He poured more whiskey into the glass, then got to his feet to cross the room and examine his face in a small mirror on the wall. It was a handsome face, he decided critically, ignoring the weakness of the mouth and the faint pouches beneath the eyes.

It was the face of a man accustomed to getting what he wanted. He meant to keep right on doing that. He was a fool to worry about something that had happened almost ten years ago. It was silly to think that anything as ancient as that could return to cause trouble for him now.

He turned back to the table. The liquor was rebuilding his confidence, and he was pleased to see that his hand was steady as he poured more whiskey into his glass. He'd be going back to Washington before long. And if that damned Quarterhill tried anything before then—well, there were ways of handling a soldier who tried to make trouble. Plenty of ways.

Faro smiled tightly.

Official ways, if he wanted to use them. The man was a Rebel who had doubtless concealed that fact when he had enlisted. That alone was enough to get him into plenty of trouble if he spoke out. And there were more direct ways of doing things if Quarterhill should try any violence. No court-martial in the world would condemn an officer for shooting down an enlisted man who threatened him with physical assault. . . .

The creak of the door as Leary, his striker, came into the room broke into Faro's thoughts. He turned his head angrily, impatient at the interruption. It wasn't that he objected to the man seeing him drink alone so much as the fact that he had told the damned fool to knock, a thing that Leary never did. He stood there now, just inside the door, with his hair falling over his stupid face as Faro stared coldly at him.

"Well, what do you want?" the officer demanded.

"Nothin', sir," the trooper said, giving Faro his vacant grin. "I just come by to see if the major wanted anything— like maybe some fresh water for his whiskey."

"Never mind my whiskey. You can rustle up some hot water for my bath if you have to do something," Faro snapped crossly. He added inconsistently, "You've taken your own sweet time about getting here . . . Where in hell have you been?"

"Over to the barracks seein' the new recruits that just come in, sir," Leary said, the slack grin still on his face. "I ain't never seen none worse, sir."

A sudden interest narrowed Faro's eyes and some of the

rasp went out of his voice. "So you don't think much of them, soldier?" he asked. "Why not?"

"They're bums, sir."

"Notice any of them in particular?"

"What's the major mean, sir?"

Faro shrugged impatiently and took down more of his drink. "Did any of them stand out from the rest?"

A pleased look came into Leary's slack face. "I reckon one of 'em did, sir. He was the one that gave the back of his hand to Corporal Clendenning on the train."

"What do you mean—the back of his hand?"

"A feller named Tash told me about it, sir," Leary said, his pleased expression deepening. "This recruit said he'd cram Corporal Clendenning's teeth right down his throat if he didn't stop talkin' about some woman on the train with them."

The comfortable feeling that Faro had experienced a few moments earlier suddenly drained out of him again. That recruit would be Quarterhill, he knew without any possibility of doubt. All the reassurances he had tried to give himself had fled, and he could feel that cold panic begin to chew at his belly once more. He had underestimated the violence of the man.

"How did the corporal take that?" he heard himself asking in a voice that didn't sound like his own.

"Oh, he's real burned up about it," Leary said with relish. "It made him look awful bad in front of——"

"Get that bath water!" Faro snapped.

The door closed behind Leary, and Faro's hand was shaking again as he added more whiskey to his glass. For a moment he had a wild idea of going to that corporal—what was his name? Clendenning?—finding the man and suggesting that he'd get official backing if he took action against Quarterhill.

No, that wouldn't do. It would only call attention to himself, link his name with Quarterhill's, and he couldn't afford that. The best thing was to get away from Fort McKeogh. That was it! There was no use taking chances.

The liquor began to bite again as a fresh thought occurred to Faro now. Lee Howell had said that she was taking the stage on to Galena Agency tomorrow. He'd offer to escort her; his orders called for him to visit Galena Agency, anyway. He'd put the thing up to old Bexar at dinner tonight. It would be the perfect excuse to get away from here, and when he returned, Quarterhill would undoubtedly have gone to join the regiment.

Yes, that was it. . . .

Corporal Clendenning ignored chow call and drank his supper in D Troop's stables from a bottle he had surreptitiously procured during his brief stay in Sunbeam earlier. Clendenning's mood became blacker as he drank. By God, he'd have to do something about that smart bastard Quarterhill! If he didn't, it was an end to the good life he'd known in this regiment. There'd be no more petty grafts imposed on unsuspecting recruits—no more bribes coming in for keeping a man's name off a duty roster . . .

The creaking of the barn door broke into his black thoughts and he heard the sound of a footfall on the soft dirt floor of the stables. That son of a bitch Harvey looking for him, he thought morosely. He slid the bottle beneath some straw.

"Who the hell's there?" he growled.

"Tash," the answer came back.

"Well, what do *you* want?"

The small man padded up in the gloom and crouched on his heels beside Clendenning. "I figured you might be here, corporal," he said with his ingratiating voice. "I figured that maybe you an' I might do each other some good."

"What the hell you mean?"

"Quarterhill," Tash said softly. "You ain't goin' to take what he done to you on the train layin' down, are you?"

"Talk plain, damn you!"

"I guess you know what I mean all right, corporal," Tash said, a smug note in his voice. "I been askin' around since I been here—talkin' with some of the old soldiers like that Garbish, for instance. They say you got a pretty good thing goin' for you with duty rosters and like that."

"So?" Clendenning asked warily.

A bland assurance came into Tash's voice. "So I figure that maybe we can make a deal. You take care of me around here an' I get Quarterhill off your back."

"How the hell could you do that?" Clendenning asked, but the rasp had gone out of his voice as a wicked interest stirred him. "He'd bust a runt like you in two."

"He wouldn't bust Mulroney," Tash said, that smug note in his voice again. "I done Mulroney a couple of favors at Jefferson Barracks. He'd do me one now—if I asked him."

"Like maybe what kind of a favor?"

"Like maybe pickin' a fight with this Quarterhill. Mulroney's an ex-pug; he's fought all of the best of 'em, he says. He'd work Quarterhill over good."

"I don't want the bastard worked over," Clendenning said savagely. "I want him crippled for life!"

"Mulroney can do that too," Tash said complacently. "You ever take a good look at his eyes, corporal? He's a killer. He fights for the love of it, and no holds barred."

"It's worth thinkin' about," Clendenning said. He fumbled in the straw and found the bottle of rotgut whiskey. He didn't need to think about Tash's proposal; he'd already decided that it was the perfect answer to his troubles. "You figure Mulroney will do the job an' keep me out of it?"

"He'll do it. How about some of that whiskey?"

Clendenning drank and passed the bottle to Tash. "Uh-huh," he said. "All right. You an' me got a deal. You're a smart little man, Tash. I ain't goin' to forget this."

"I don't figure you will," Tash said complacently. "I told you Mulroney's a friend of mine, didn't I? He wouldn't like it if you didn't take care of me, corporal. Now that we understand each other, when you want this job done?"

"Tonight," Clendenning said viciously.

Supper was over and Melrose, the acting supply sergeant, herded the recruits back to the supply room at the rear of the barracks and issued them clothing and equipment: arms —saber and Springfield carbine and Colt revolver—saddle gear and horse accoutrements, overcoat and poncho, two blankets and a bed tick to be filled with straw for a mattress.

"Lose any of it and you'll find it on your payroll," Melrose said sourly. "All right, get it stowed away."

Quarterhill carried the stuff back and dumped it on his bunk, took the bed tick, and went out to the straw pile by

24

the stables to fill it. Coolness had come into the evening, and this was good he thought. He was glad that he had come back to this. In a way, it was as if he had never been gone.

He came back into the long barrack room with its floor of pounded earth and the double row of bunks stretching along its length. A coal-oil lamp hanging from the ceiling gave out a dusty yellow light. The recruits who'd ridden with him from Jefferson Barracks were clustered in little groups, sorting out the unfamiliar equipment. He saw that Corporal Clendenning was sitting with Mulroney in a corner, their heads together. Both looked at him as he came in—then glanced away.

Mitch Garbish was standing by the door of the orderly room. Now he sauntered forward and sat on the bunk opposite Quarterhill's while he smoked a cigar and watched with bright, interested eyes as Quarterhill set about making up his bed and stowing away his gear with the ease of long practice.

"You handle that little chore of work like you'd done it before, Reb," Garbish said lazily. "Not that it's none of my business, you understand."

Quarterhill paused almost imperceptibly, shooting a glance at the ex-sergeant's seamed face. It was blandly innocent. That "Reb" could have been pure chance, Quarterhill decided; or it could have come from the trace of Georgia drawl that still crept into his voice now and then.

"It's none of your business," he agreed, but his voice was not unfriendly. "Anything else on your mind?"

"A drink," Garbish said regretfully. "It's a frivolous thought, friend Quarterhill, with payday two weeks off and the sutler with no more heart in him than a chunk of rock when it comes to extendin' beer credit to a gallant soldier boy."

Quarterhill finished stowing the last of his stuff in his wooden locker and straightened. He liked what he had seen of Mitch Garbish. The man had a wry humor in him, and Quarterhill suspected that, despite the marks of hard living on him, the man was a competent soldier when it suited him to be.

"A glass of beer wouldn't be bad after a hard day, Mitch," he murmured. The name came easily to him. "If an ex-sergeant does not mind drinking with a recruit, I might stand you one."

Pretended shock showed on Garbish's square face. "Will miracles never cease," he said. "A recruit with money on him! I will accept your kindly offer, Reb."

Quarterhill got his stiffly new campaign hat and fitted it to his head, and together he and Garbish went out into the soft dusk and turned along the row of barracks. Lights glowed across the parade ground in the windows of the officers' quarters, where anxious wives held the home front while their husbands were away on the Powder. The barracks were dark and silent.

"There is a great lonesomeness to a post when the regiment has gone, friend Quarterhill," Garbish said. "It is like a thing with the spirit gone out of it, and only the corpse left. There should be mourners."

Quarterhill glanced at the man beside him. "And how is it that you're not gone with the regiment?" he asked.

"Ah, that is a long story there," Garbish said in a pleasantly reminiscent tone. "A sad story, friend Quarterhill. A story that has a lady in it—one of the belles of Sunbeam and no better than she should be, it comes to me now. There was a matter of a few drinks and this and that was goin' on when her husband come home unexpected. He was upsot and hollered for the guard patrol. They come on the run, and when the smoke had cleared away, the guard patrol had sundry black eyes and loose teeth and Garbish had lost his sergeant's stripes and was in the can for thirty days. This time the colonel did not relent, and the regiment marched away without Garbish. No good will come of it."

Quarterhill chuckled. "A sad story," he agreed. "When did they let you out, Mitch?"

"Day before yesterday, friend Quarterhill," the other said. "Just in time to nursemaid a herd of fool recruits from Sunbeam out to the fort. It was no job for a soldier of my qualities. You do not wear the look of a recruit. You have worn the uniform before, or I have never seen a soldier."

The last was unexpected, taking Quarterhill a little off his guard. He did not answer for a moment and they walked along in silence, the end of Garbish's cigar glowing in the deepening darkness. Garbish was the first to speak.

"Tell me it is none of my damned business, friend Quarterhill," he murmured. "I will not take offense."

"I have soldiered before," Quarterhill said quietly.

"In the war, perhaps?"

"In the war."

Garbish let his breath go out gustily. "I saw my share of it," he said. "Havin' no better sense, I was in the infantry then. I will say to you that it is no way to fight a war. First Bull Run to Appomattox, and I walked the whole damned way of it. It was more than a million miles . . . and we will speak no more about it, friend Quarterhill."

"A long way," Quarterhill murmured. "A long, long way —and a long time back."

The barracks and the stables and the quartermaster sheds and warehouses were behind them now. They came presently to the sutler's store, a low building made of logs. Inside was a long room with a plank bar running the length of one side of it. A coal-oil lamp hung from the ceiling, and aside from a dour man behind the bar, the place was empty.

"A very good evenin' to you, MacIntosh, you old skinflint," Garbish said cheerfully, leading Quarterhill up to the bar. "And how is all the money in your moneybags tonight?"

The sutler, a gaunt man with a drooping mustache, looked at Garbish without pleasure. "If you're aimin' to ask for credit, ex-Sergeant Garbish," he said in a rusty voice, "you cannot have it. As to my moneybags, they are all right."

"Credit!" Garbish dismissed the thought with a wave of his hand. "My friend here is buyin'. Do you shake hands with Recruit Quarterhill, MacIntosh, and set out two beers."

The sutler jerked his head dourly at Quarterhill, brought the beers, then retired to the end of the bar to lose himself in a tattered and much-thumbed newspaper. Garbish lifted his glass and squinted at Quarterhill with bland good humor.

"Mud in your eye, friend Quarterhill," he said. "You are welcome to Fort McKeogh. May all of your women be faithful and all of your fights lucky."

"A man could not ask for more," Quarterhill answered, lifting his own glass. "*Salud*, Mitch."

He drank and put the glass down. The front door creaked

with a faint complaint and boots scraped on the boards of the floor as Quarterhill turned his head a little to look. One of his fellow recruits, Mulroney, stood there at the edge of the lamplight, his head tipped forward a little as he peered around the room from beneath his hairless eyebrows.

Quarterhill scarcely knew the man. He had exchanged words with him perhaps a dozen times during the two weeks that they had been together at Jefferson Barracks and en route here, he supposed. Mulroney was a surly man who kept to himself—an ex-prize fighter, so the rumor went. Quarterhill could believe it. The other was squat and heavy-set, and his small eyes peered belligerently from a red face that was heavily marked with scars. Now he moved toward the two at the bar with a curious, rolling gait, his fisted hands held low and swinging across the body. His eyes were fastened on Quarterhill as he came.

He halted directly in front of Quarterhill. "I have come for a fight, dandy," he said, his voice growling deeply from his thick throat. "Put up your hands."

Quarterhill turned so that his elbows were hooked over the edge of the bar as he looked dispassionately back at Mulroney, his eyes watchful. The man was sober, he saw— not drunk, as he had thought at first. A little bell at the back of his mind alerted him. Something lay behind this that was not apparent on the surface. He and Mulroney had no quarrel.

"Why?" he asked mildly. "You and I have nothing to fight about, Mulroney. Why not forget it?"

Mulroney stamped his left foot hard twice on the floor and cocked his fists as he watched Quarterhill from beneath his naked brows. "Put up your hands, bucko!" he said impatiently. "Fight, man! I will not hit a man with his hands down!"

Out of the corners of his eye Quarterhill saw that Garbish was standing quietly by, his face alert and interested. He returned a strict attention to Mulroney.

"Give me a reason, Mulroney," he said, his voice expressionless. "I do not fight without a reason."

"Ahhh," Mulroney said, expelling his breath violently. "You would have it so, dandy!"

He swung a big fist at Quarterhill's head, moving with

28

surprising speed for his squat build. Quarterhill, expecting something like this, pulled back just in time and felt hard knuckles graze his chin. He rocked forward and drove his own left fist deep into Mulroney's belly—heard Mulroney's breath explode in a coughing grunt. Mulroney came back, crowding Quarterhill hard against the bar, and Quarterhill felt an agonizing stab of pain as the other stamped a vicious heel into his instep.

He wrestled free and slugged Mulroney twice in the roll of flesh beneath the man's ear. Then one of the ex-pug's swinging blows caught Quarterhill high on the head and he went over backwards, crashing into a table and rolling to the floor. It was like being kicked by a mule, he thought fuzzily. Mulroney was coming toward him, and from the way he moved, Quarterhill knew that the other was about to drop both knees into him with rib-shattering force. At the last second he rolled.

Mulroney hit the floor—was up again like a cat. Another blow caught Quarterhill in the face just as he was coming to his own feet, and he went down again. Dizzily he saw that Mulroney was coming on to stomp him with his heavy boots. Sudden understanding flooded through Quarterhill as he rolled a second time.

The man means to kill me, he thought in that fleeting instant. *This is no fight. He'll kill me or cripple me so bad that I'll never walk again. Why? Why?*

A killing anger of his own surged through him as he evaded Mulroney's rush and came back to his feet. *If that's the way he wants it,* he thought savagely, *that's the way he'll get it!* He sidestepped the next rush and dug a fist viciously just below the ex-pug's rib cage. A rusty voice assaulted his ears.

"That's enough of it. Stand still, both of you!"

It was MacIntosh, the sutler. He stood behind the bar, his mouth thin beneath the scraggly mustache and his eyes angry. A sawed-off shotgun was in his hands and its twin muzzles covered the two men in front of him.

"Take your damned fights elsewhere," he said flatly. "I will not have you breaking up my furniture or giving me a bad name with the colonel. Get out—all of you!"

Mulroney stood in the lamplight, his hands hanging at his

sides. For a moment he stared at Quarterhill with his pale eyes. Then he turned abruptly and went through the door with his rolling gait. There had been no expression on his face.

It was the face of a man who came to do a job, Quarterhill thought. *It was nothing more and nothing less.*

"What the hell was *that* all about, friend Quarterhill?" Garbish was asking. "Don't he like you?"

"I don't know," Quarterhill said shortly.

They went on back through the night toward the barracks, not talking. Quarterhill felt spent and empty, his face hurting where Mulroney's knuckles had scraped it. Garbish was busy with his own thoughts. He spoke at last.

"I would keep lookin' back over my shoulder for that one," he said. "I do not think you have seen the last of him."

3

"A Man's Past Is His Own"

The twilight was deepening as Jacob Miller neared the set, a little larger than the rest, which was Colonel Felix Bexar's quarters at the end of the line. Bexar met him at the door. The colonel was a small, gravelly-voiced man made cantankerous by old wounds and the arthritis in his joints.

"Come on in, Miller," he said. "Faro's not here yet. . . . The women are doing whatever the hell it is that women do before supper. We've got time for a drink in peace and quiet."

"Thank you, sir," Miller said.

They sat in the colonel's study, a place made bright with Indian blankets and comfortable with rawhide chairs. The colonel's striker brought whiskey and cigars. At Bexar's gesture, Miller mixed himself a weak drink and sat back, enjoying the aroma of one of the colonel's cigars—a treat after the cheap stogies that were all he could afford on a first lieutenant's pay. Bexar lighted his own cigar and blew a cloud of smoke in front of him.

"Glad you could come," he growled.

Miller smiled faintly. "My social calendar isn't exactly crowded with engagements these days, sir," he murmured.

Bexar ignored that. "It'll be a pleasure to have somebody to eat supper with besides Faro. Listening to him tell how important he is back in Washington ruins my appetite."

"I have done little more than pass the time of day with Major Faro since he has been here," Miller said, eying the ash on his cigar. "He has more important things than first lieutenants on his mind. At least that has been my impression."

Bexar snorted. "If he has a mind behind that recruiting-poster face of his," he said. "Just between you and me, Jake, the fellow's a conceited ass and I've just about had my belly full of him, by God! I'll be glad when he's gone."

"Just why did he come here, sir?" Miller asked.

"To snoop is my guess."

"Sir?"

"His orders say that he is looking into Indian affairs for Major General Rufus H. Romney," Bexar said sourly. "Translated, that means that the wolves are just about to catch up to *that* crooked old son of a bitch, and he's sent Faro out here to find a goat that he can shift the blame onto to save his own skin. I know Romney—it's the sort of thing he would do."

Miller nodded soberly. He knew what Bexar meant, for the papers lately had been full of stories of the congressional investigation into Indian affairs. It was an unsavory mess, and General Romney, attached to the Indian Bureau in Washington, seemed to be in it right up to his ears.

He asked quietly, "Why would Major Faro think that he can find a goat here, sir? Hat, and his braves on the Galena reservation, have been quiet for better than two years."

"A lot of unrest has been building up there, just the same," Bexar grunted. "I have no doubt the rumors have gotten back to Washington. If Hat should jump the reservation this summer, it would take the heat off Romney—transfer it to the people out here. He would be off the griddle. They would be on it."

"You and Colonel Howell?"

Bexar cocked a sardonic eye at his lieutenant. "Who else?" he growled. "We're handy, ain't we?"

A faint flush crept up beneath the tan on Miller's thin face. "By God, sir, they can't get away with that! You and Colonel Howell at the Galena Agency have kept Hat quiet for two years. Don't they know that back in Washington?"

"They know it," Bexar said grimly. "You forget that Washington is a city of politicians, Miller. A politician's first duty is to protect his own mangy hide. Right now they're scratching like hens in a manure pile to find cover for themselves." Bexar stopped and stared moodily at the end of his cigar.

Miller stirred a little in his chair and took another small sip of his whiskey. The worried lines deepened in his thoughtful face as he looked back at the other man. Jacob

32

Miller had a vast affection for this cantankerous colonel. The thought that he might be the victim of Washington intrigue, after all of his long years of service, disturbed the lieutenant.

"You mentioned disaffection, colonel," he said after a moment. "Do you really think that Hat might jump the reservation—move north and join the Teton Sioux?"

"I wouldn't bet that the old bastard wouldn't try to do just that," Bexar said grimly. "I had a letter from Sam Howell yesterday. Both he and the Indian agent, Grimes, are worried. Hat's young braves have been increasingly insolent around the Agency. Somebody is stirring them up, Howell thinks."

"Would the regiment's being gone have anything to do with it, do you think, sir?"

Colonel Bexar's face darkened. "What do *you* think?" he demanded in a dour voice. "That's just another example of the pig-headed thinking back in Washington. That goddamn' peacock Gilmorin has to sprinkle a little more glory on his feathers, so he sells the War Department on a show of force in Montana to keep the tribes up there quiet. As a result, *my* regiment moves two hundred miles north to join his goddamn' show on the Powder, and I'm left here with a corporal's guard to keep Hat in line. The whole lousy, fouled-up business makes me want to puke!"

"I guess I can see why," Miller said.

Bexar shrugged and stamped the fire out of his cigar. "Don't let it bother you too much, Jake," he said, his voice softening a little. "You're getting out of here Thursday morning. Leave it behind you. By God, you've earned it!"

"I hate to go at a time like this," Miller said, the worry coming back into his face. "You'll have no officers here—line officers, that is—except Viercy commanding the infantry detachment. I could ask for a delay in reporting—"

"Don't be a goddamn' fool, Jake!" the old man snorted angrily. "The Army's given you nothing except the privilege of eating dust out here on this goddamn' frontier for twenty years. Now that you've got a chance at something better, you take it and run like you had the devil at your coattails!"

"Fiddlesticks on your coattails," a voice said tartly from the doorway. "Come on out of that lair of yours, Felix

Bexar. Major Faro is here and supper is waiting. Good evening, Lieutenant Miller. So nice of you to come."

Lucy Bexar stood there in the doorway, her smile taking any sting out of her words. She was a small woman, gray-haired and with a warm vitality about her. She had kept her figure, and her complexion was almost girlish, despite the eight years of wind and sun that she'd known here on the frontier. Her eyes were tender and sympathetic as she saw pain reflected in her husband's face when he lifted himself out of the chair.

"Coming, coming," Bexar said grumpily, but his expression eased a little as he looked at his wife standing in the doorway. "Never run a man's coattails down, Lucy. They're the only things he can call his own these days."

They moved into the square parlor. Mark Faro stood with Lee Howell by the big stone fireplace, Miller saw. There was something faintly possessive in the way the major bent toward the girl, he thought; there was something that was a little predatory in the man's darkly handsome face. It was the face of a man who would boast of his conquests, it occurred to Miller as he went across the room. Well, it was none of his business.

"Good evening, major," he said quietly. "It is a pleasure to see you again, Miss Howell."

Mark Faro dominated the talk at the table. The man had charm, Jacob Miller had to admit to himself. He listened, taking little part in the conversation and conscious of the poor figure that he must cut beside this man who knew all the ins and outs of society in Washington City. Colonel Bexar also ate largely in silence, his eyes brooding. It was near the end of the meal that Miller realized, with a little confusion, that Faro was addressing a question to him. Faro's expression was bland but there was a mocking light in the major's eyes that put Jacob Miller suddenly on his guard. Faro's voice was casual.

"I have been meaning to ask, lieutenant," he said. "What was your service during the war? Army of the Potomac?"

Miller's eyes turned hard as he looked across the table at the other. He was well aware of the difference in their ranks; he was also well aware that Faro was probably ten years younger than he was and that Mark Faro probably had been graduated from West Point well after Jacob Miller was there. It was apparent that the question was meant to enhance Faro in Lee Howell's eyes at Jacob Miller's expense. Miller was suddenly angry.

"I served throughout the war here on the frontier, major," he said thinly. "My misfortune, perhaps."

"Oh," Faro said and let the silence hang for a moment while he pointedly avoided looking at Miller's shoulder straps with the bars of a first lieutenant. "Well, I suppose they had to have somebody here on the frontier."

"I suppose they did."

Lucy Bexar frowned a little as she sensed the tension that was building up. "I think that perhaps those who served out here had the hardest service of all, major," she said gently. "It had all of the dying but none of the glory."

A faintly sour expression crossed Faro's face for a brief moment. It was gone almost as soon as it had come, but Felix Bexar, sitting at the head of the table, had not missed it. *Good shot for you, old girl,* he thought, glancing affectionately at Lucy out of the corners of his eyes. *About time that this fellow got taken down a peg or two.*

"I take it that you served with the Army of the Potomac, major," he said blandly. "That qualified you for Washington, I imagine. Experience and ability, eh?"

Faro laughed deprecatingly. "Oh, I wouldn't put it quite that way, colonel," he said, but there was a trace of smugness in his voice. "Of course, I *did* see a good bit of the war; I was fortunate enough to end up as a brevet colonel when the war was over. I got the breaks, of course."

"I believe that you have mentioned it before," Bexar murmured. "What general were you aide to, major?"

A faint flush crept into Faro's dark face, and for a fleeting instant, Miller saw the vindictiveness that crept into the other's eyes. He remembered what the colonel had said about Faro's probable mission out here, and it worried him again as he sensed the smoldering anger in the man.

"General Phil Marston, sir," Faro was answering smoothly, however. "I don't believe I mentioned being his aide, before. You must be clairvoyant, colonel."

"No clairvoyance," Bexar said drily. "I happen to know the Army, is all. Aides go up faster than others." Faro's

35

flush deepened and the colonel abruptly changed the subject as he turned to Lee Howell. "Young lady, what are your plans about going on to the Galena Agency? I would strongly recommend that you stay on here with Lucy and me until your father can escort you out there. That has the added virtue that it would give Sam an excuse to pay us a visit. It would be pleasant to see him."

Lee Howell's eyes met Miller's briefly as she turned her head to look at Colonel Bexar. There had been understanding in that brief glance, Miller thought. He was grateful for it, and at the same time it made him a little angry.

"Lucy said that the weekly stage leaves tomorrow for Galena, Uncle Felix," Lee was saying. "I think that I had better take it. After all, I have been gone for three months now; it's time that I got home and took care of Dad."

"Imagine he's been able to muddle through," Bexar grunted. "Still, once you women get it into your heads that a man has got to be looked after, he's going to be looked after. I wish that I might send an officer escort with you. I cannot. The chuckle-heads in Washington have taken my regiment away from me."

"Colonel Bexar," Lucy said firmly, "that is no way to speak of Washington in front of your guests."

Bexar leered genially at her. "Now, Lucy," he said, "I'm being polite about this. You should hear some of the names that I've got for Washington when I'm really in form."

"Tut, I don't care to hear them, Colonel Bexar."

The colonel turned back to Lee. "Of course, you'll be in no danger, young lady," he said. "There are night stops at Doxy, Jensen's Ranch, and Harney Creek. Still, I would feel better in my mind if one of my officers was accompanying you."

"I shall be quite all right. . . ."

Faro broke in and Miller saw the quick calculation in his eyes. "You can set your mind at ease on that score, sir," he said. "As you know, my mission takes me to Galena Agency anyway. I'll be most happy to escort Miss Howell."

Sergeant Major Ed Harvey, sour with an old man's early-morning crankiness, came into D Troop's orderly room and sat down behind the first sergeant's desk. Sergeant Melrose, the acting supply sergeant, followed him into the room and hoisted a hip onto a corner of the desk as he squinted at Harvey with amusement in his eyes.

Harvey glowered back. "Well?" he demanded.

Melrose eased the gimpy leg that would not let him ride and had kept him here after the regiment had gone. "You look like you'd had a fight with your wife this mornin', Ed," he said. "If you had a wife, that is."

"Thank God I ain't," Harvey growled. "I've got all of the trouble I can handle now."

"Now, where would a sergeant major find trouble?"

Harvey glowered at him. "It is not enough," he said, "that I've got to act as first sergeant to all of the misfits that are left on this post now that the regiment is gone. The lame and the halt in hospital, the jailbirds in the guardhouse—not to mention a baker's dozen of fool recruits who don't know their left foot from their right. No, that is not enough. Early this mornin', before Reveille has yet gone, I've got to scare up a wagon and a team of mules and a driver to take Miss Howell to the stage in Sunbeam. Which same I do not mind doin', you understand, Melrose, for Miss Howell is a fine young lady."

"What the hell you beefin' about then?"

"I've also got to see that the wagon and the team of mules and the driver goes to the quarters of this Fancy Dan major from Washington and loads up *his* baggage."

"You mean Faro?"

"I don't mean nobody else. It's a pity that Washington doesn't keep its majors to itself but has to send them out to bother hard-workin' soldier folk."

"That Faro is a bad one," Melrose said reflectively, getting a plug of tobacco out of a pocket and worrying off a chew. "I knew a guy like him in Chicago once—had the same look in his eyes. This feller was a bouncer in a whorehouse . . . handsome bastard. Like Faro. He'd put a knife into you so slick that you'd not know you'd been cut until you was dead."

"I wouldn't trust this major we got no further than I could throw him," Harvey agreed sourly. "He has a mean streak in him. I was helpin' to load his baggage into the wagon when I drop a cowskin bag that he has got. He damned me up one side and down the other like I was a recruit."

"Maybe it had whiskey in it," Melrose suggested practically. "Man could get real upsot if you dropped his whiskey bag. What's Faro gettin' his baggage loaded for?"

"He's escortin' Miss Howell to Galena Agency," Harvey said morosely. "Which is the same as no escort at all. Go find the recruit Quarterhill, Jake. Say to him that I wish to see him here and that he'll lose no time reportin' himself."

Quarterhill came after a few moments, and Harvey let him stand at a loose attention in front of the desk while he surveyed him with a frosty eye. Then he reached for the service record in front of him and jerked his head.

"Shut the door," he said. "An' set down."

Quarterhill closed the orderly-room door—and came back to sit on a hard chair beside the desk while he gave Harvey a noncommittal and unbothered regard. The sergeant major scowled at the service record and tossed it back on the desk.

"Quarterhill," he grunted, swiveling his eyes like gun barrels back to the other's face. "That your right name?"

"It's my right name," Quarterhill said.

"Your record says naught of previous service," Harvey went on in his gritty voice. "But I was not born yesterday. You have worn the uniform before. Am I right?"

"Maybe," Quarterhill said.

"The cavalry arm?"

"Maybe."

Harvey grunted and gave Quarterhill another hard look out of his frosty eyes. "A man's past is his own," he grumbled. "It would be my guess, if I was to guess, that you once wore a uniform of a different color. That is neither here nor there. Are there any sheriffs lookin' for you?"

"Nary a sheriff," Quarterhill told him.

"A wife, maybe? Or two?"

Quarterhill grinned a tight, fleeting grin. "No wives either, sergeant. I have been lucky that way."

Ed Harvey seemed not to hear him as he scowled dourly at the wall. "Once in a hell of a long time," he said, "a man comes along that a noncommissioned officer, such as myself,

38

thinks—just thinks, mind you—might be made into a soldier. I had that thought about you last night."

"I appreciate the compliment," Quarterhill murmured.

"Not so goddamn' fast with your appreciation," Harvey retorted sourly. "That was before I heard that you were fightin' with the recruit Mulroney in the sutler's store last night. Do you deny that you were, recruit Quarterhill?"

Quarterhill's eyes turned hard as he met Harvey's stare. "I do not deny it," he said.

"Why?"

"He braced me. We fought."

"And why did he brace you, recruit Quarterhill?"

Quarterhill moved his shoulders slightly. "Ask Mulroney, sergeant," he said. "I do not know."

Harvey's weathered face settled into deeper lines. "So the ex-sergeant Garbish said that you told him," he said, his tone a little more mild now. "You have known this man Mulroney somewhere before, perhaps?"

"I set eyes on him fust at Jefferson Barracks a little more than two weeks ago."

"You had trouble with him there?"

"None. We spoke perhaps a dozen times."

Harvey scowled and sat back in his chair, studying Quarterhill with his pale gray eyes for a long moment. "The ex-sergeant Garbish told me another thing, Quarterhill," he said at last. "The ex-sergeant Garbish says it is his belief that recruit Mulroney meant to cripple you bad—maybe to kill you. Garbish is a great liar, but not that great. Do you agree with what he thinks?"

Quarterhill shrugged again. "That is another thing that I do not know, sergeant," he said. "Perhaps."

"And why would he want to do that?"

"Ask him," Quarterhill said once more.

"I mean to do that," Harvey said grimly. "I have doubt I will get any answers that satisfy me."

Quarterhill agreed with that doubt, but he said nothing. He had asked himself these same questions. Remembering the look he'd gotten from Mark Faro there on the depot platform, he'd wondered briefly if Faro had taken this way to get rid of a man who could ruin him, but he dismissed the idea as being wholly improbable. Faro would not dare take that chance. It was much more likely that Clendenning was the clown hidden in the woodpile. He did not voice that thought to Ed Harvey. If it proved to be so, he would take care of it in his own way, and it would be well taken care of.

"I will find my answer in time," Harvey was saying softly from across the desk. "I cannot stop two men from fightin' when they wish to fight. I would not if I could. But from now on you will do your fightin' off the post. Is it clear?"

"It's clear," Quarterhill said, getting to his feet. "Will that be all, sergeant?"

"For now," Harvey growled. Quarterhill started to turn but Harvey's voice stopped him. "This man Mulroney is a bad one, so Garbish says. I have my ways of attendin' to such. I do not think that he will brace you again."

Quarterhill saw the reserve in Harvey's face and his own eyes hardened. "Save yourself the trouble," he said thinly. "I do not need others to fight my battles for me."

"Ah," Harvey said, a pleased satisfaction in his voice. "I did not think that you did. That is all, Quarterhill."

Corporal Clendenning talked with Tash in a corner of the stables. The dark-brown taste of rotgut whiskey was still in the corporal's mouth, and his throbbing head made his temper even shorter than usual this morning. He looked sourly at the smaller man in the dim light that came from the door.

"A hell of a fighter your trained seal Mulroney turned out to be," he said savagely. "I told you I wanted that damn' Quarterhill crippled, and the bastard has got scarcely a mark on him to show for it this morning, by God!"

"Take it easy, corporal," Tash said, a faint whine replacing the usual urbanity in his voice. "I told you how it was. That damn' bartender busted things up with a shotgun. Don't worry none. There'll be another time. . . ."

" 'There'll be another time,' " Clendenning mimicked sourly. "Maybe there will and maybe there won't. Quarterhill will be on his guard now, and that son of a bitch of a Harvey suspects something. We made a bargain and you fouled me up. I got a good notion to take it out of your hide, by God!"

"Now, wait a minute, corporal. . . ."

Clendenning swung around viciously, his throbbing head goading him. "Wait," he said, the sarcasm heavier in his voice. "Yeah, I'll wait—I can't do nothing else now. But you come through or you'll find your name on plenty of duty rosters, by God!"

"Don't worry. I'll come through, corporal."

4

Provisional Q Troop

Recall from drill finally sounded and the recruits, Quarterhill among them, thankfully broke ranks in the slanting sun of the late afternoon and straggled back toward D Troop's barracks. Quarterhill felt the tiredness in all his muscles, long unused to this sort of thing, but it was a good tiredness, he thought. It was the tiredness of a long day's work put in at the chores he remembered and felt at home doing.

He washed off the sweat and grime, taking his turn under the crude shower behind the barracks. As he came back into the long, dim room, a towel wrapped about his middle, he passed Mulroney, who was seated on his bunk. The squat man got up and followed as Quarterhill moved on down the aisle.

He stopped at the end of Quarterhill's bunk, looking at him with no expression in his pale eyes for a moment. Then he said abruptly, "The next time we fight, dandy, do you hold your guard a little higher. I have no wish to kill you."

Quarterhill had climbed into his underwear; now he reached for his shirt. "The next time we fight, Mulroney," he said quietly, "my guard will not matter to you, because I will break you into two pieces. If I were you I would remember that."

"We will see," Mulroney grunted impatiently. "Be sure that there will be a next time. Then we will see."

He stamped impatiently on down the aisle. Corporal Clendenning put his head and shoulders into the doorway at the far end of the room. His voice was petulant and surly.

"All right! All right! Snap it up, you birds! Fall in outside for Retreat, God damn it!"

The recruits, joined by a score of other casuals—men released from the guardhouse and hospital after the regiment had gone, headquarters and post personnel left behind for housekeeping duties, a few others—formed in a double rank at the edge of the parade in front of D Troop barracks. Ed Harvey, acting first sergeant, took the reports; that done, he looked over the motley detachment with his customary frosty stare.

"At ease," he said. "Them that want passes to town tonight will see me after Retreat in the orderly room. Details for tomorrow's guard an' cook's police are posted on the bulletin board. See that you check 'em."

A voice said, "Sergeant, can I ask a question?" Quarterhill recognized Tash's faintly whining voice.

"Ask," Harvey said.

"Can the recruits have a pass?"

"Recruits do not go on pass," Harvey told him dispassionately. "If you do not have enough to do tonight, recruit Tash, cleanin' your carbine and polishin' your other gear, I will see if I cannot find something else for you to do."

"I just asked," Tash said in a surly voice.

"And you got answered," Ed Harvey said thinly. He glanced over his shoulder toward headquarters, where the field music had assembled and the details were at the flagpole and the saluting gun, then swung his attention back. "Detachment . . . ten-shun!"

Quarterhill pulled heels together and stiffened his legs. He felt a warm stirring deep inside him. It was a long time since he had last stood Retreat, he was thinking. Faint memories of evening parade back at West Point returned to him.

This frontier post—with its baked parade, its graceless line of officers' quarters unshaded by any trees, its ugly headquarters building set against a dun background of hills, its Suds Row and its barracks and stables—was a far cry from the green plains of West Point. Yet, as the silvery notes of the trumpets lifted, sounding Retreat into the coming evening, he knew that Fort McKeogh and West Point, beneath their outer trappings, were the same. They stood for something, but they were more than symbols. They were solid things that a man could tie to. . . .

The saluting gun coughed out its cloud of white smoke

43

and the hills tossed back the echo of its sound in diminishing waves. The field music began to blow "To the Colors" as the flag came down, a splash of color against the brassiness of the sunset. Unconsciously, Quarterhill stood a little straighter.

The trumpets held on one last, lingering note. It died and Sergeant Major Harvey kept his right hand at the brim of his campaign hat for the space of a breath, then dropped it to his side. He faced about, giving the detachment a final crusty glance before letting it go for the night.

"Dismissed!" he said.

First Lieutenant Jacob Miller sat in Colonel Bexar's office at headquarters and listened absently as the last notes of the trumpets died away. The colonel's orderly had summoned him here a few minutes ago. Miller saw, by the dark and angry expression on Bexar's face, that trouble had arrived.

The colonel abruptly hurled the stub of his cigar at a cuspidor and swung around to face Miller squarely. "All hell's broke loose, Jake," he said. "Hat's left the reservation, taking his women and children with him. I got a dispatch by courier from Sam Howell at Galena an hour ago. Sam thinks that we're in for trouble—real trouble. I agree with him."

"How long has Hat been gone, sir?"

"The best part of two days," the colonel said soberly. "Sam thinks that he's headed for a place called Ghost Basin up beyond the headwaters of Fourth of July Creek. I understand that's bad country up there. Do you know it?"

Miller's thin face grew thoughtful as he spread the map of this country out in his mind. The memories of countless scouts, of little skirmishes, of lone patrols, fitted themselves neatly into place, and Ghost Basin fell into the slot where it belonged. The colonel was not wrong. It was bad country.

"I know it, sir," he said. "It's this side of the divide between the headwaters of the Fourth of July and the headwaters of Loon Creek. Not much of a basin—just a hole in the hills protected by heavy stands of timber. Elk winter there, I've been told, when the snow gets too deep in the Galenas."

"How long a march from here, Jake?"

Miller considered that soberly. "Two days to Jensen's

Ranch and the Sleepy Wind," he said carefully after a moment. "Another two days up the Fourth of July to the divide. Say four days in all—if you're lucky."

"God damn it, Jake, I can't give you four days!" Bexar exploded violently. He stopped and got hold of himself with an effort and his voice was milder as he resumed. "You've got to be in Ghost Basin, ready to fight with whatever troops you can gather up, by Saturday morning. You have *got* to!"

"Sir?"

Colonel Bexar let his breath go out gustily. "All right," he said. "Last night I told you that you'd be a goddamn' fool if you didn't get out of the country when you had the chance. That still stands. I'm asking you to stay a little longer. I can't order you to do it. Technically you're no longer under my command. You can tell me to go to hell if you want to . . . I wouldn't blame you if you did. I hope you won't."

The expression on Miller's sober face didn't change. "Let's get on with it, sir," he said.

There was affection in the glance that Bexar shot him but the colonel's voice was harsh and businesslike as he went on. "All right. Today is Tuesday. Tonight you will form a provisional troop from whatever odds and ends of cavalrymen you can lay your hands on here at McKeogh. You will march tomorrow at daybreak and be in Ghost Basin, prepared to fight, by Saturday morning. It doesn't matter that it can't be done. You have got to do it, Jake! A hell of a lot could depend on it."

"Maybe you'd better tell me, sir," Miller said quietly. "All I know now is that Hat's off the reservation."

Bexar thrust a paper impatiently toward him. "Here . . . it's Sam's dispatch. Never mind; damn it to hell, I'll tell you myself! He and Grimes, the Indian agent, have reason to believe that Hat's on his way to a big powwow with other dissident bands—probably Tetons coming from the north. They figure that this powwow will take place in Ghost Basin on the eighth—that's Saturday. Well, that powwow must *not* take place!"

"No," Miller said quietly. "Colonel Howell and Grimes are sure of their information, sir?"

"Sure enough so that they'll meet you at Jensen's Ranch

45

day after tomorrow—accompany you up the Fourth of July," Bexar said. His voice turned bleak. "Sam and Grimes think they can persuade Hat to return to the reservation. I don't think they can. If Hat refuses to treat, Jake, I want you to scatter his band and bring him back here in arrest—or packed head down across saddle. I don't give a goddamn which. Is that clear?"

"It's clear, sir."

"We're skating on thin ice," Bexar went on heavily. "Hat may be planning to make medicine up there in the Basin that will turn everything north of the Sleepy Wind into one great-big bloody bonfire. That's what comes of letting that glory-hunting bastard steal my regiment away from me!"

"Can you get reinforcements?"

"I have wired for infantry to come by rail. They will get here sometime tomorrow, and part of them will follow you up Fourth of July Creek. They will never get to Ghost Basin by Saturday morning, Jake. You will have to do the job with what you are able to scrape up here tonight."

"Yes," Miller said absently, his mind already busy with the things that had to be done. "I will mount every man who can stick on a horse and fire a gun, colonel."

Bexar arose heavily. "Report to me tonight—no matter what the time—when you are organized," he said. "I have given you an impossible job. You can still tell me to go to hell."

Jacob Miller had no answer for that; it was typical of him that he did not have an answer. He was a soldier; there was soldiering to be done. He would do it, and there would be no quibbling about it. He got out of his chair.

"We'll make out, sir," he said. "I'll be on my way now. One thing—I would like to take Sergeant Major Harvey along as first sergeant of the provisional troop."

Colonel Bexar's smile held affection again. "You didn't have to ask, Jake," he said. "Good luck to you. I only wish to God that I was going along with you. I can't. An old crock like me would only slow you up."

The coal-oil lamp above the desk burned with a smoky light from a badly trimmed wick as Jacob Miller sat in D

Troop's orderly room and made his final plans. It was after midnight as the door opened and Ed Harvey came in, the creases deeper in his weathered face. He turned out his careful salute.

"I've got thirty-eight men, sir," he reported, looking at a paper in his hand. "Includin' all that were in the guard-house, them in the hospital that are well enough to ride, the clerks from headquarters, the trumpet tooters and the drumbeaters from the band, and all the recruits that has fired a gun or sat a horse. It will be such a troop as would turn your head gray, but at least each has got two arms and two legs."

"Good," Miller said tightly. "What about noncoms?"

"A rub there," Harvey said. "Melrose we cannot take. An hour's hard ridin' and his leg would be busted all over again. There is Clendenning, but he is not much. I would put the stripes back into Garbish, but he will not take them."

"Why not?"

Harvey moved his shoulders slightly. "He is a contrary man, lootenant. He says to a private he was busted and a private he will stay. I would not let it worry me, sir. Stripes or no stripes, he will be there when we need him."

"Anyone else?"

"There is a recruit," Harvey said thoughtfully. "I have mentioned him to the lootenant before—a man by the name of Quarterhill. He has soldiered, and soldiered well, before— I would not mistake the signs, sir. It is my recommendation that you make him a lance corporal, lootenant."

"Done," Miller said. "Inform him, sergeant."

"I will that. He is a good man."

Miller nodded. "We are going to need good men, Ed," he murmured. "What about ammunition?"

"I have seen to it that each man has sixty rounds for his carbine—twenty for his pistol, sir."

"Good. Rations for six days?"

"Rations for six days."

"We will ride hungry coming back," Miller murmured. "But the reduced weight will help us to get there faster, and we will need that help. We can do no more tonight. Turn in, Ed. Tomorrow will come too soon, I think."

"Aye, tomorrow always comes too soon," Harvey said. "I will have one last look around. Is the lootenant takin' his own advice about turnin' in, sir?"

"After I make my report to the colonel, sergeant. He is waiting up for it."

When Jacob Miller walked across the empty parade ground, the moon had come up. Its pale light lent an eeriness to the sleeping quarters and the sagebrush-covered hills that rose behind them. Miller thought with a little regret of the train that he would not be taking on Thursday morning. He put the thought away from him. There would be other trains.

A tiny thread of worry came into his mind as he remembered that Lee Howell had left for Galena Agency this morning—no, that was yesterday morning now. Anyway, she would be stopping at the Doxy stage station tonight. Perhaps, if Colonel Howell had left the Agency as his dispatch had indicated, he would be at Jensen's Ranch to meet her tomorrow evening. Hat would already be into the hills. His worry was probably unfounded.

Its little nag remained, though.

A light burned in Colonel Bexar's quarters, and Bexar opened the door to Miller's knock. The old man was dressed in a faded bathrobe, his shanks bare, as he led the way into his study. A bottle of whiskey and glasses were on a low table.

"A nightcap will do us no harm while you make your report, Jake," the colonel said. "Sit down, boy, and pour yourself a good one. You are ready to move?"

Miller nodded. He poured whiskey into a glass and left it neat as he sat down. "We'll march out at first light, sir," he said. "Those are my orders."

"How many men?"

"Forty, counting Harvey and myself. Not too bad, considering. We'll push hard—hope to reach Jensen's Ranch around noon day after tomorrow—push on up the Fourth of July that afternoon. By marching most of Thursday and Friday nights we should reach Ghost Basin by daybreak on Saturday."

"A long march, and a hard one," Bexar said soberly. "And

the pickings and leavings of the regiment to do it with. I wish you luck, Jake. You're sure to God going to need it."

Miller took his drink down and put his glass back on the table. "No more, sir," he said in answer to the colonel's gestured invitation. "If there are no further instructions, I'll be getting along. I still have a few things to do."

Bexar walked with him to the door and put a hand on the younger man's shoulder for a moment. "I wish to God that bastard Faro was still here," he said violently. "He'd be heading up the Fourth of July . . . and you'd be taking the train for West Point if he was, and Washington be damned! Well, he ain't."

"It's all right."

"I suppose. Take care of yourself, Jake."

"I'll do that, colonel."

Walking down the line in the moonlight, Jacob Miller wasn't so sure. He was not an imaginative man, but he had a feeling tonight that he had never had before on the eve of riding out of Fort McKeogh. It was late, but he'd write to his mother before he turned in, he decided. It wasn't time yet for his monthly letter, but it never hurt to be on the safe side. . . .

Reveille went at three-thirty, and men turned out in the darkness, spitting and hawking and swearing as they assembled in front of D Troop's barracks. Ed Harvey called the roll, reading his roster by the light of the lantern that Trooper Wheelding held for him. Harvey's voice was crusty.

"Atkins!"

"Here."

"Laduel"

"Hyar."

Harvey finished and slipped the roster back into his pocket. "Get your breakfast," he said. "Quarterhill, report to me in the orderly room. Dismissed!"

Webb Quarterhill was waiting in the sickly light of the lamp as Harvey came in. Harvey stood in the doorway for a moment, his eyes surveying the younger man with their customary glacial chilliness. Then he moved on behind the desk with deliberate tread and sat down in the chair that was there.

"Set down," he growled testily. "Yesterday mornin' I asked you if you had soldiered before. You did not choose to give me an answer one way or another. That right?"

"That's right."

Harvey nodded curtly. "I said to you then that a man's past is his own, and I will leave it so." He paused for a moment while his eyes bored into Quarterhill. "Still, I've got opinions of my own, and I've also got to make a purse out of a sow's ear by kickin' this bunch of bums into a troop. I've got to have help in doin' it. You are Lance Corporal Quarterhill as of now . . . and if you happened to of learned your soldierin' in a gray suit, I could not care less, Lance Corporal Quarterhill."

Quarterhill sat quite still for a moment, the lamplight flooding across the sober brown planes of his face. Then he moved his shoulders slightly and gave Harvey a tight grin.

"Under those conditions, I accept," he said.

"I spoke naught of conditions," Harvey grunted, his temper edgy and sour from morning coffee still unsettled in his belly. "You will take your orders from me and the lieutenant, Miller. You will carry them orders out as a noncommissioned officer should. If you do not, I am as like as not to have you stood up and shot. Is all that quite clear, Lance Corporal Quarterhill?"

"It's clear," Quarterhill murmured, a hint of amusement still in his voice. "Would it be asking too much, Sergeant Harvey, to inquire what this is all about?"

"It would," Harvey growled crustily. "I will tell you all the same—although it is little enough that I know, myself, about this thing. We march this mornin' for the Sleepy Wind and Fourth of July Creek to put the fear of God into a dog-eatin' Sioux chief by the name of Hat. He has jumped the Galena Reservation, makin' signs like war, and has headed for Ghost Basin, which is at the headwaters of the Fourth of July."

"It is a long march?"

"Four days. We will make it in three, Lance Corporal Quarterhill. Does that scare you?"

"You've said that I have marched before," Quarterhill answered evenly, getting up. "It does not scare me, sergeant."

50

Dawn was beginning to put its first streaks of light into the eastern sky as the motley crew that made up the provisional troop led their mounts out into the chill of the morning. Horses grunted and stamped uneasily; men talked in the surly monotones of people whose sleep has not been long enough and who face the prospect of the coming day without enthusiasm.

Mitch Garbish walked beside Quarterhill as the two moved toward the troop assembly area, their horses plodding behind them. The shapes of the barracks and the stables were beginning to take on substance as the light grew.

"It is an ungodly hour for a man to be stirrin' about, friend Quarterhill," Garbish said, with faint malice in his voice. "It is the hour, by God, when a man should be turnin' over and pullin' the blankets about him for another snooze— or maybe reachin' out for the woman beside him."

"I wouldn't know," Quarterhill said.

"Ah, wouldn't you, now?" Garbish's voice was skeptical. "Well, take my word for it—it is. And a hell of a sad thing, too. Would you know what this is all about? Somebody must of got a flea in his ear in a goddamn' hurry to turn us out like this."

"A Sioux chief, named Hat, has jumped the reservation and is headed for a place called Ghost Basin," Quarterhill murmured. "It seems that we are to go after him and put the fear of God into him and such of his braves as he may have along, Mitch. That is the general idea, anyway."

"The sweet Christ in the foothills," Garbish said, genuine shock in his voice. "The fear of God, you said?"

"That's right."

"You must of been eatin' opium, friend Quarterhill. The bunch of misfits that we got couldn't put the fear of God into a lame tabby cat. If the tabby cat was to spit at them, they would run like the devil was on their coattails."

There was a faint amusement in Quarterhill's voice as he answered. "You wouldn't be running down the fine men of Q Troop, would you, Mitch?" he asked. "They are hand-picked."

"They are hand-swept, you mean," Garbish grunted. "Ed Harvey swept 'em out of every dark cranny where a no-good could hide himself . . . the bums out of the guardhouse . . .

51

the malingerers out of the hospital. Headquarters clerks with two left feet—not to mention two heads . . . What is it with this Troop Q that you mention, friend Quarterhill?"

"There was a story during the war," Quarterhill said, his voice suddenly a little wary, "that the Confederates had such Company Q's among their cavalry. At first they were made up of men who had lost their horses. Later on, the name was given to AWOL's, stragglers, men who drew rations but did not fight. . . ."

"Then I will say that Q Troop is a good name for us," Garbish said glumly. "Well, here we are."

Ed Harvey's gravelly voice cut through the low mist that clung to the parade ground. "Stand to horse! Prepare to mount. . . . Mount! Sir, the troop is formed!"

Lieutenant Jacob Miller's voice came back. "Take your post sergeant. Column of fours. Walk . . . hoooh . . ."

5

The Attack on Jensen's Ranch

The stage road, fetlock-deep in the July dust and meandering through the foothills as it sought the easiest grade, climbed finally to a low bench that roughly paralleled the course of the Sleepy Wind. Lee Howell, deeply powdered with the dust that had been pumped up by the racketing wheels of the stagecoach during the long day, looked out of the window at the crimson sheen of the sunset on the river. Major Mark Faro rode beside her, his handsome face turned sulky by the heat and the discomfort, and by the disinterest that Lee had shown during the last hour for his reminiscences of the pleasures of Washington City that the two had shared during Lee's brief visit there a year ago.

The road swung around a stand of lodgepole pine, and Faro could see a cluster of buildings on the flat top of the bench half a mile away—a solidly built log house and outbuildings and a corral. The driver urged his tired teams into a trot.

"I suppose that is Jensen's Ranch ahead," Faro said in a halfhearted effort to resume conversation. "A grim-looking place. Why would anyone want to live out here, I wonder?"

Lee controlled her irritation with an effort. She and Mark Faro had been the only passengers since the stage had left Sunbeam yesterday morning. At first she had found the major's conversation witty and amusing; she had genuinely enjoyed living over the few times that they had been in each other's company in the East. After a while, however, the man's conceit and arrogance had begun to show through his flowery words, and today she had ridden utterly bored with Major Mark Faro.

"They live here because it is a living, I suppose," she answered, her voice a little sharper than she had meant to make it. "Or perhaps they love the country. It has a wild beauty to it, I think. Why does anyone live anywhere, major?"

"People who live out here are fools," Faro said crossly. "They are only half civilized."

"Does that include me, Major Faro?" Lee asked, a gentle barb in her voice. "*I* live out here, don't forget."

Faro's face darkened and he let go of the grab strap for a moment to gesture with his left hand. "Of course it doesn't include you, Lee—Miss Howell," he said. "You're Army. I meant anyone who lived out here by choice."

"I am not sure," Lee murmured as she turned to look at him, her eyes thoughtful. "Perhaps if I had to make a choice, I would choose to live here, Major Faro. I rather think that I prefer Wyoming Territory, with all of its wildness, to the grubbiness and cheap intrigue of Washington City."

"Damn it," Faro said, petulance suddenly thinning his voice, "we've been riding together for two days—we will ride together for two days more before we get to Galena Agency. My name is Mark! Do you have to be so confounded formal?"

Amusement crept into Lee's eyes now. "Why, no, Mark," she said. "Not if it will make you feel any better."

The stage was pulling into Jensen's now, the driver slowing his teams to a walk as they went by a pole corral and a wagon shed. He slammed on the brakes and the coach came to a halt in front of the log house. A squarely built man, wearing the blue of the United States Army, stood on the little porch under its wooden canopy. Lee Howell sat for a moment, her mouth a little open, then she was down into the dust unassisted and running with her head thrown back and her arms out.

"Dad! Dad!"

Colonel Sam Howell came down off the porch to meet her halfway, his expression a mixture of gladness and worry. "Lee!" he said. "I didn't expect you for a week yet."

"I wanted to surprise you," Lee told him. "And, if you didn't expect me, what are you doing here at Jensen's Ranch to meet me, you old fraud?"

Howell disengaged her gently to lead the way inside the house, the big room dim in the dying day. "I'm not here to meet you, Lee—though thank God that I *am* here, now

54

that you've come," he said soberly. "Hat is off the reservation; small war parties of his braves have already begun raiding along the Sleepy Wind. You must return to Fort McKeogh tomorrow."

"And you, Dad?"

"I sent a dispatch to Felix Bexar to send all of the troops that he could scrape together at McKeogh to meet Grimes and me here at Jensen's," he said. "They won't follow the stage route but will move across country and should be here sometime tomorrow. When they get here I mean to go after Hat."

Lee ironed out the sudden worry that had come into her face; she forced herself to show a serenity not reflected in her eyes. Mark Faro came into the room, followed by Old Man Jensen and his son-in-law, Spiney, who was carrying the bags.

"Be careful of that cowhide bag, my man," Faro said curtly to Spiney. Then he saw Colonel Howell in the shadows and came toward him, hand outstretched. "Ah, Colonel Howell. It's nice to see you again, sir. Faro. Mark Faro. I met you when you were in Washington a year ago. I've had the pleasure of Lee—Miss Howell's company on the stage from Sunbeam."

"Yes, yes," Howell said absently, dropping Faro's hand. "Remember you. Had a letter from the Department about you coming out here. Doing something for Romney, aren't you?"

"Yes, sir," Faro said, his tone stiffening at the absence of any particular cordiality in Howell's greeting. "General Romney feels that there are certain aspects of Indian affairs that need looking into out here, so he sent me. . . ."

"General Romney is a little tardy in his interest," Howell said, his voice suddenly harsh. "Thanks to him, and other fools like him in the Indian Bureau, we may have a wholesale war on our hands out here in a matter of days, sir!"

Faro's dark face flushed and a vindictive expression came into his eyes. "I do not care to hear General Romney called a fool, colonel," he said stiffly. He recovered himself quickly as he shot a glance at Lee, beside her father. "But such official matters can wait until we reach the Agency——"

Howell cut him off abruptly. "Major Faro," he said in a

cold voice, "right now you are not going to the Galena Agency. You can either accompany Grimes and me in pursuit of Hat and his band, or you can return to Fort McKeogh on the stage. It is immaterial to me which you choose to do."

"Pursuit of Hat?" Faro asked stupidly.

"Precisely," Howell said, clipping his words. "Hat left the reservation three days ago, taking his women and children with him. That is a bad sign. It could mean that he is seeking an alliance with the northern Tetons for some concerted move against the whites in this territory."

"That's impossible!" Faro said. "When I left Washington there was no hint of an Indian uprising."

"Washington is a long way from here, sir," Howell said coldly. "If it were not, it would know about the crooked traders out here who have been selling whiskey and guns to the Indians. It would know about the dishonest contractors who have been growing rich supplying the Indians inferior goods on government contracts—at least, I hope it would know about them, Major Faro."

"Are you implying something, sir?"

Howell didn't answer for a moment as he stood with his feet a little apart and his hard glare on Faro. "Major Faro," he said softly at last, "I pray to God that Washington is merely blind and stupid in this matter. I pray that it has not known of conditions out here all along and, for reasons of its own, has deliberately closed its eyes to them!"

Thursday morning dawned with a blood-red sunrise at Jensen's Ranch. Mists still hung over the willows and alder that hid the banks of the Sleepy Wind as Old Man Jensen and his slow-moving son-in-law and Barkley, the stage driver, loaded baggage back onto the stagecoach and brought out the teams to be hitched. Major Mark Faro, his dark face sour and brooding, left the log house and picked his way carefully through the dust, pulling his gloves on as he went. He came to the coach and waited.

He'd refused Howell's invitation to accompany the expedition up Fourth of July Creek after Hat. He'd said stiffly that he had to get back to Fort McKeogh and the railroad, where he could get in telegraphic touch with General Romney and ask for fresh instructions. He hadn't missed the skeptical look

56

that crossed Howell's face as the older man heard the explanation. That was riding Faro with a set of rough spurs now.

"The goddamn' mealy-mouthed old bastard!" he said to himself under his breath now, the two Jensens and Barkley being busy with the teams. "He might just as well have come right out and accused me of being afraid to go! Well, let them hunt their goddamn' Indians; that's not my job!"

It was a good, sensible explanation, he knew; he was sullenly angry that it wasn't a wholly satisfactory explanation—even to him. He wished now that he had taken a little more from that bottle before he had put it back with the others in the cowhide bag. God damn it, he was a fool for not having slipped the bottle into his pocket. If he wanted to take a a little nip now and then in the stage, it was nobody's business but his own. If the Howell woman didn't approve, to hell with her! He hadn't been getting to first base with her, anyway, since her old man had appeared on the scene. To hell with the whole goddamn' bunch of them!

Howell and Lee came from the house, walking slowly toward the stage, Lee's hand on her father's arm. The driver spat tobacco juice into the dust, climbed over the wheel to his high seat, and began to gather up the reins. The sun tipped the mountains to the east, flooding the narrow valley of the Sleepy Wind with radiance and burning off the last of the mist.

Faro straightened as Lee and her father reached the stage. He bowed coldly to Howell, neglecting to salute, climbed into the coach, turned, and reached a hand down.

"Permit me," he said stiffly.

Lee Howell seemed not to notice. She turned abruptly and put her arms around her father's neck and pulled his head down for a long kiss. Mark Faro waited awkwardly with his hand outthrust for a moment longer; then he withdrew it and seated himself sulkily at the far side of the seat.

"You'll be careful, Dad," Lee was saying huskily. "Promise me that you will."

"Of course." Howell laughed, but there was little mirth in the sound. "Nothing to worry about, Lee. We will talk Hat into returning to the reservation with his people, and that will be the end of the whole affair. You just sit tight with Lucy and Felix for a little while and have a good visit."

He handed her into the stage. The driver kicked off his brake and flicked a rein smartly against the flank of the off-wheeler. "Hup, Bess! Git into it, you crowbaits!"

Howell stood waving as the stage turned out into the dusty track, turning to retrace the route it had followed yesterday. Lee leaned out of the window, her head turned back as she waved good-by with a handkerchief. Her father was lifting an arm in answer just as the first yells and shots came from the trees at the back of the ranch house where a small gully came up from the flats. She saw Sam Howell slump to his knees in the dust.

The stage made a convulsive leap forward as the driver lashed his teams into a run. Faro's hands were on Lee now, dragging her back inside the coach. Barkley's voice drifted shrilly down to the two, anger and fear in it.

"Injuns! God Almighty Christ!"

Lee lay back against Faro for a moment, her face white and her lips pressed tightly together. In that instant before the major had pulled her away from the window she had seen a dozen half-naked riders, heels dug into the flanks of spotted ponies, explode out of the shallow gulch and go careening toward the ranch buildings. Their wild whoops still filled her ears.

With a vast effort she fought down the panic that tried to rise in her—the nausea that filled her throat. She was dimly aware that the stage was swaying crazily as the wheels bounced over the rocky tracks; out in front the spooked horses, bits in their teeth, were running out of control with bellies to the ground as they swung into the partial shelter of the stand of lodgepole pine. Lee clawed her way to the window again.

"Turn back!" she screamed at the driver. "We've got to go back and help them! Turn around, damn you!"

The wind whipped her words away—she might as well have been screaming at the moon. Faro's hands reached for her once more, his clawing fingers tearing her dress and digging into her flesh as he pulled her back against him on the seat. She fought viciously against him in silence, aware that his face had taken on the dirty color of old putty

58

and that terror had put an animal wildness into his staring eyes. He flung her roughly back against the seat, holding her there.

"You little fool!" he panted, his voice almost unrecognizable. "Do you want to be killed—scalped?"

"Make him turn back! Make him!"

Faro's voice rose. "No! We have to outrun those devils back there! It's our only chance!"

"You coward! Oh, you dirty coward!"

The words cracked like a slap in the face, but they made no impression on Mark Faro. He had gotten a stubby derringer out of a pocket now and was crouched on his knees between the coach seats, holding Lee down with his left arm across her as he waved the gun wildly in his right, first at one window and then at the other. All reason had left him.

Up above them, Barkley gave up trying to control the wildly running horses and knelt in his seat, peering to the rear with his own gun in his hand. Half a dozen braves were in pursuit through the scattered lodgepole pine, which raced by on either side of the swaying coach. They came on, a quarter of a mile back, bent low over the necks of their racing ponies and firing as they came. The gap was closing too fast.

"See if I can't discourage that," Barkley mumbled. "The bastards are gettin' too close for comfort."

A bullet screamed off the top of the stage, exploding a shower of splinters into his face as he spoke. He rested his left forearm along the back of the seat and laid the long barrel of the Colt across it as he tried to time the coach's lurches. It wasn't much good. He fired twice, missing both times. His pursuers had cut the distance in half now.

"You ain't got many more chances," he told himself. "An' you ain't goin' to have no time to reload."

He waited patiently, trying to align his bobbing sights on one of the riders a scant two hundred yards behind. A third shot missed, then a fourth. Barkley cursed violently, the profane words more like a prayer. If it was, it was answered, for as the powder smoke of his fifth shot blew clear, he saw a running pony go down, flinging its rider over its head in a bone crushing fall. Barkley fired his last shot, then dug at his belt with frantic fingers for fresh cartridges. It wasn't necessary.

The remaining pursuers were hauling up now and were circling back toward the Indian, who lay where he had fallen. Barkley let his breath go out in a long, windy sigh as he faced to the front again and reached the flapping reins.

"Ah," he said aloud through his heavy mustache. "God an' the Lady Luck are with you today, Bill Barkley. . . ."

The words died, choking in his throat, as a heavy fist slugged him between the shoulder blades, driving him face down across the boot. He hung there for a moment, arms working feebly, then slid on down to strike the tongue of the stage and carom off it beneath the flying hoofs of the off wheel horse. The stage's iron-tired wheels passed over him but Bill Barkley never knew it. He was dead before he ever touched the ground.

The horses, further maddened by the firing, increased the speed of their stampede. The lodgepole pine on either side kept to the road as the swaying stage careened dangerously. Inside the coach, Lee fought her way back to sanity. The firing had stopped but the mad flight continued, and something had happened to the driver, she knew. She looked at Faro, still waving his useless derringer, and understood that she'd get no help from him.

This time he made no effort to stop her as she pulled her way back to the window and worked the upper part of her body through until she could see forward to the driver's seat. It was empty. The teams were running out of control. They had almost reached the end of the bench now, and she remembered that here the road dropped steeply into a winding dry wash.

"Help me!" she called back to Faro. "The driver's gone and the horses are running away! We've got to get them under control before we hit the wash!"

Faro sat stupidly on the floor, his eyes glassy as he looked up at her without answering. The sight sent hot anger running through Lee. How could she ever have found this man attractive, she wondered dully as she tried to pull herself through the small window and get a hand on the baggage rail on top.

After what seemed like an eternity, the groping fingers of her left hand finally closed over the metal rod. With a silent prayer Lee loosened the grip of her right hand on the side of the coach window, pushed herself outward, and reached upward. The coach lurched toward her side so that she was thrown free and, for a brief instant, dangled there in space, sustained only by her hold on the railing on top of the stage.

Then the stage lurched back in the other direction and she was slammed against its side with a force that drove her breath out. Somehow she managed to hang on and get a foot up into the window. With snail-like slowness she inched herself up until she was lying, face down, on top of the stage at last. Lee clung there for a moment, getting her breath; then crawled forward to slide down into the empty driver's seat.

"Oh, my God!"

The words were forced out of her involuntarily as she saw that it had all been for nothing. The reins, which had slipped from Barkley's nerveless fingers, were trailing in the dirt beneath the hammering hoofs of the runaway teams.

Lee sat frozen in the seat. Like a person in a dream, she watched the last of the lodgepole pine race toward her. The bench ended and the careening stage whirled into the steep downgrade as the road entered the dry wash. The pace became even faster, and the stage bucked and rocked like a ship in a heavy sea now. It couldn't last, but somehow it did as Lee clung to the seat.

They were on the floor of the wash, the road twisting and turning as it followed the gulch's curves. A mile fled behind them—another. The horses were tiring now and their pace was slowing a little. Lee wondered if she dared venture out on the swaying tongue of the vehicle; perhaps she could get hold of the bits of the two wheel horses and bring them under some sort of control. They were nearing the point where the road left the wash, and on the upgrade they might slow enough for her to do it.

But the runaway teams, still galloping blindly, did not take the road where it swung to the right to climb out of the gulch. They continued straight ahead, and in that instant Lee knew that it was all over. A reaching rock snag cleaned the spokes out of a front wheel and the stage tipped down with a crash.

Lee was flung from her seat to somersault through the air. In the split second before she lit she knew that the trace hooks had snapped and that the teams, free of their dragging load, were stampeding on. The coach lurched crazily and then went over on its side, skidding into the brush with a great cloud of yellow dust. That was the last thing that Lee knew.

She struck heavily on her side and agonizing pain ran through her like a knife before merciful darkness came to blot everything out. Overhead a buzzard wheeled lazily in the cloudless sky as the morning grew into day.

Back on the bench at Jensen's Ranch, Marie Jensen and her two daughters—one of them Spiney's wife—still held out in the log ranch house, barricaded against the Sioux raiders, who were content to take their time now. Spiney, shot through the shoulder with an arrow but still able to handle a gun was with them. He had been nearest the house when the first rush had come and had been able to make it inside. The others had not been so lucky.

Old Man Jensen had been killed by the barn. Grimes, the Indian agent, had died by the corral and lay there, face up in the sun, half a dozen spiteful arrows shot into him after he had taken the bullet that had killed him. Colonel Sam Howell, mortally wounded at the first fire, had managed to stay on his knees in the dirt, shooting back, until a painted warrior had raced by, leaning low from his pony, and split the colonel's head with a war club. Overhead, buzzards were gathering here, too.

Smoke, followed by licking flame, came from one corner of the barn. Off to one side the haystack went up in flames. Marie Jensen, a stern-faced woman, took command in the ranch house. Spiney didn't mind; he was used to taking orders.

"The soldiers will be here sometime today," Marie Jensen said harshly. "We'll hold out until they come—if those red devils don't burn the house down on us first."

"You think they will, Maw?" Spiney asked.

Marie gave him a cold look. It didn't much matter, she

thought, with Jensen lying dead and scalped out there by the barn. Still, she couldn't cave in now.

"I don't think nothing," she said flatly. "Josie, have a look at your husband's shoulder. He ain't worth much, but he's one more gun and we need all we can get."

A muffled shot, coming from the kitchen, echoed dully through the big room, and the voice of Sue, the younger of the Jensen girls—a pretty kid just turned sixteen—followed it.

"Maw, more of 'em are coming up out of the gully! A whole pack more of 'em!"

"I'm comin'," Marie Jensen said.

6

Skirmish at Black Rock Crossing

Troop Q (Quarterhill's name had spread and caught on) was astir at 3 A.M. on Thursday morning, the second day of the march from Fort McKeogh. Lieutenant Jacob Miller talked with Ed Harvey in the starlight as he shaved with cold water, grunting a little as the razor pulled at his beard.

"We didn't cover enough distance yesterday, sergeant," Miller said curtly, interrupting himself to swear as the razor nicked him. "Not enough by far. We'll have to almost double that today if we're to reach Ghost Basin by Saturday morning."

"Yes, sir," Harvey said glumly. "We will that. I'm puttin' Lance Corporal Quarterhill in charge of the point today, lootenant, instead of Corporal Clendenning. That may help."

"He seems to be a good man," Miller grunted. "You think that Clendenning held us up yesterday?"

"He didn't pull us along none," Harvey said in a sour tone. "He rode with his head over his shoulder, stoppin' to check out every sign no matter how old it was. We got no time for that crap if we're goin' to get to the Basin by Saturday."

Miller wiped his razor and stowed it in his saddlebags, then dried his face on the tail of his shirt. The skin of his face burned as if it were on fire, and that added to his early-morning disillusionment with things in general.

"Caution has its uses," he said, keeping his feelings out of his voice. "Right now we've got to sacrifice caution for speed. Quarterhill is new out here. He doesn't know the country. Do you think it is wise to put him on point?"

"He may not know the country, but he knows war," Harvey replied heavily. "Of the two, the last is more important in my book, lootenant. The ex-sergeant, Garbish, will be with him. *He* knows the country. It is enough, I think."

"All right," Miller agreed, buttoning his shirt. "Hurry the men along at their breakfasts. We move in half an hour—be lucky if we get to Jensen's by midafternoon."

Harvey found Webb Quarterhill squatting with his squad by a small fire made of sagebrush roots. Mitch Garbish, the red glow of the coals on his stubbled face, cooked bacon; boiling coffee set its fragrance into the morning. For a moment Harvey stood there in the shadows, not speaking.

He knew these men and he was weighing the worth of each before he made his presence known. Besides Quarterhill and Garbish there were five of them: young Clay Atkins, a headquarters clerk until yesterday morning; Ladue, the French Canadian who'd been awaiting trial in Fort Mc-Keogh's guardhouse for knifing a Sunbeam gambler; A hare-lipped trooper named Hess who seldom spoke; Samp Dolliver, the Yankee from Maine; and Amen Jones, a quiet and solemn man who rode with a Bible in his pocket. None of them, for one reason or another, had been deemed fit to ride with the regiment.

A hell of a collection of warriors, Ed Harvey thought sourly. They were led by a man of whom he knew little but suspected was an ex-Confederate, and *he* was seconded by a careless rowdy who had had his stripes taken away for too much drink and too many other men's wives. A hell of a goddamn' Army!

Harvey shrugged and moved forward until the faint glow of the dying fire lighted the craggy lines of his face. "Hurry it up," he said roughly. "This ain't no Delmonico's where you dawdle about your eatin'. Quarterhill, a word with you!"

Quarterhill came to his feet with a long, easy movement and the two of them stepped a little apart in the starlight. Early-morning snortings and the uneasy trample of shod hoofs came from the picket line. The low murmur of voices, bad-tempered in the damp and chill of approaching day, made an undercurrent of sound. Quarterhill had heard it all before more times than he could well remember, he was thinking.

Harvey halted, and for a moment the two didn't speak as they listened to the splash of the river and looked at the mountains looming over them in the dimming starlight. Harvey broke the silence at last with his gravelly voice.

"You and your squad will be point for today's march, Lance Corporal Quarterhill," he said. "I will expect you to see that the march gets on faster than it did yesterday. We have not got the rest of the year to get to Ghost Basin in. We will be there by Saturday mornin' if we have to march the rest of the way without a stop. Is it clear?"

"Clear enough," Quarterhill murmured. "How about a little thumbnail sketch of the country ahead, sergeant?"

"You would be happier without it," Harvey grunted. "It may be that there is worse country to cross than goin' up the canyon of the Fourth of July—if so, I have not heard of it. Until we reach the Fourth of July the goin' is not too bad."

"Up the Sleepy Wind?"

"Aye, once we reach the river. We will hit it at the Black Rock Crossing—ford it there and follow up the valley to the Jensen Ranch, where we will pick up Colonel Howell and the Indian agent, Grimes, if things go accordin' to plan."

"How far from there to the Fourth of July?"

"A matter of four miles along the flats. We will ford the river again below the mouth of the canyon."

"We won't camp at Jensen's, I take it?"

"We will not," Harvey agreed sourly. "Unless Colonel Howell should say that this whole thing is a mistake and that we do not go after Hat after all. I do not think he will say that. So we will go on. The Fourth of July joins the Sleepy Wind a matter of three miles or so upriver from the ranch."

"I've got it," Quarterhill said. "Anything else?"

"Nothin'," Harvey said. "Except that you keep movin'. We'll be in hostile country once we cross the Sleepy Wind, with Hat on the loose. Don't let it worry you none."

"I've been in hostile country," Quarterhill murmured. "And we'll keep moving, sergeant."

Half an hour later the column was on the march again, Webb Quarterhill and his five men half a mile out in front. Lieutenant Miller rode at the head of the column. Somehow he felt old this morning. An uneasy depression rode his shoulders and he tried without success to shake it away. He

66

had a feeling that nothing good was going to come of this day. He wasn't wrong.

Quarterhill's point reached the Black Rock Crossing early in the afternoon. Mitch Garbish, riding ahead, came to the river and halted while he waved Quarterhill up. The lance corporal came at an easy lope and reined his horse up beside the other.

"What's up?" he asked sharply.

"Nothin' that I can see," Garbish answered. "It's what I don't see that bothers me, friend Quarterhill. There's a smell to this place that I don't like."

No skepticism showed in Quarterhill's lean face. He knew what Garbish meant; he had been in too many fights to ignore even such a nebulous warning. The river ran broad and shallow here, clear water sparkling over the gravel bottom. On the far side a small flat, perhaps two hundred yards long and half of that wide, was dotted thickly with willow and alder as it screened the mouth of a small, steep-sided canyon which led back into the foothills. Right and left were slopes covered with sagebrush, its drab grayness relieved by the splashes of color that lupine and Indian paintbrush made. Quarterhill gave the canyon his brooding attention, his face settled into thoughtful lines.

"If Hat has got any war parties roamin' around, they could not find a better place to ambush the troop than right here," Garbish was saying. "They'd catch them heroes of ours while they was all spraddled out crossin' the river."

"My thought," Quarterhill agreed absently. "Well, there is one way to find out if there are any Sioux hidden over there. Go across and see, Mitch."

Garbish gave Webb a wry look out of the corners of his eyes. "Yeah," he said. "I could of figured that out for myself, friend Quarterhill. So here goes nothin'."

He kneed his horse forward, but Quarterhill's voice stopped him. "Hold it up, Mitch."

The rest of the point was coming up now except for Atkins and Jones, the two flankers. Quarterhill waved them in. A quarter of a mile back he could see the small dust cloud that marked the approach of the rest of the troop, men and horses still hidden by the high sagebrush. His five reined their horses up.

"Garbish and I will go across," Quarterhill said curtly. "Cover us. If nothing happens, the rest of you follow one at a time. We'll cover you from the far bank."

Quarterhill watched while the others dismounted and pulled carbines from saddle buckets; then he nodded and he and Garbish pushed their horses forward into the water. It was belly-deep at midstream, where Quarterhill's horse picked its way carefully against a current that was stronger than it looked. Quarterhill rode tense, his ears waiting for the sound of a shot and his body braced against the sudden impact of a bullet.

Neither came, and presently he and Garbish were walking their horses through the shallows and into the shelter of the willows, which came down to the water's edge here. Garbish moved a few yards to where he could cover the upstream approach and dismounted, his carbine in hand. Quarterhill waved an arm and saw Ladue start across. Three hundred yards away, on the far side of the Sleepy Wind, he saw sun glint on metal as the rest of the troop came on. He rejoined Garbish.

"Easier than I figured," Garbish said. "Maybe too easy. What do you think?"

"That there's no Indians here," Quarterhill said drily. "Or that they're looking for bigger game."

"I'll take it, whichever way it is," Garbish murmured. "I never did like being shot at."

The point was assembled on the flat now and it resumed its march formation, but a small warning bell kept ringing in Quarterhill's ears as he rode. That steep-sided canyon that came out of the hills back at the crossing bothered him. On a sudden impulse he whistled a shrill command to Garbish and the flankers to halt, and waved them back in. As soon as they had rejoined, he led the way into a small gully that climbed at right angles to the flat. It was choked with brush. They followed it for fifty yards; then Quarterhill dismounted them, left Atkins to hold the horses, and took the rest in a steep climb to where a small knob overlooked the crossing and the canyon that worried him.

"Get yourselves positions where you can cover anything

coming down the canyon," he ordered curtly. "I've got a feeling that trouble will come out of there."

It was a good position, his practiced eyes told him. There was cover and a good field of fire for the carbines. The lead files of the troop were approaching the crossing now; he'd not have long to wait. Garbish settled beside him.

"You smell something, Reb?"

"Call it a hunch."

"Harvey will have a fit that he ain't got a point out if nothin' comes of this," Garbish said philosophically. "It will be the skin off your own backside, my friend."

"It's *my* own backside," Quarterhill grunted.

And nothing was going to come of it, he was beginning to think as the last of Q Troop straggled out of the river and bunched up on the willow flat. It was in that moment that disaster struck. A Sioux war party, not too large—perhaps twenty-odd warriors—came out of the canyon like a hurtling cyclone and slammed into the momentarily disorganized cavalry below. Quarterhill caught a confused glimpse of horses rearing wildly, of riders being unseated, of a great boil of dust down there below.

"Fire slow and pick your targets," he heard himself yelling. "Don't hit our people!"

Now the carbines began to speak with authority from the knob, putting their spiteful cracks into the afternoon. His men were behaving well, Quarterhill noted with satisfaction; they were showing a steadiness greater than he had hoped for. The surprise of aimed fire from the knob was having its effect. A couple of riderless Indian ponies whirled away. A part of the troop had rallied from its first panic and was dismounted and firing back now. The pressure of the crossfire was too great for the Sioux to take, and suddenly it was all over.

The war party was streaming upriver through the willows, their shrill hoots drifting back. Quarterhill's small party sped them on their way with a few parting shots. Then the raiders were out of range and the attack was over.

Beside Quarterhill, Garbish got to his knees, his expression sour as he looked at the confusion that still reigned down on the flats. Quarterhill could hear the angry rasp of Harvey's voice as the first sergeant booted stragglers out of the brush and tried to restore some sort of order to the command again. He could see Corporal Clendenning bustling about importantly down there, accomplishing little, he suspected.

"A hell of a fine band of heroes we got," Garbish was saying disgustedly. "Maybe twenty braves in that bunch, but they hooraw half of our valiant fightin' men into the brush and they scare a year's growth out of the other half. It is with them that we are goin' to put the fear of God into Hat, Reb?"

Quarterhill moved his shoulders slightly, his face betraying nothing. But he had been thinking much the same thing, he had to admit to himself. He'd been thinking also that with Q Troop Lieutenant Jacob Miller was going to have to be like Joshua and command the sun to stand still if he was ever to get to Ghost Basin by Saturday morning. Well, it was none of his affair.

He sifted dirt through his fingers, delaying for a moment to let things get a bit straightened out down there before he went below and made his report. Mitch Garbish was still fuming over the disgraceful behavior of the troop.

"It's the first time that most of them have ever been shot at, Mitch," Quarterhill murmured. "It's a small excuse. A man never knows what he will do when he is first shot at. Can you remember when that first happened to you?"

"I cannot," Garbish answered. "There is too many years in between, friend Quarterhill. Too many drunks and too many women. I never think back. There is no pay in it. That does not make me any happier with the bunch that we got down there. It is as fine a collection of guardhouse bums, goldbricks, hayseeds, and wife escapers as I ever laid eyes on."

"You have them classified," Quarterhill murmured, a faint amusement in his voice now. "Into which class do you figure you and I fall, Mitch?"

Garbish gave him a bright glance out of the corners of his eyes. "Ah, it is a good question, friend Quarterhill," he said. "At least we wear a little of the soldier's mark on us— you and me. It is not much, but it is something."

"Yes," Quarterhill answered absently. "Hold the men here on the knob, Mitch, in case some of Hat's people decide to sneak back for another try. I'm going down below and see what's what. I'll be back presently."

He got to his feet and moved to the left toward the gully where they'd left the horses. Garbish watched him go, a faint affection in his eyes. Ladue, the French Canadian, got up from where he was squatting and came to join Garbish. He hunkered down, worrying a chew from a plug of tobacco as he did so.

"Where's he goin'?" he asked, not caring.

"Down below," Garbish said lazily. "Where the hell did you think he was goin', Frenchy? To a Maypole dance?"

"I don't think," Ladue grunted. "If I did I wouldn't be in no goddamn' army or out on no goddamn' picnic like this."

"What's wrong with this?"

"I don't like it," Ladue said, spitting. "There ain't nothin' about it I like—goin' off on a wild goose chase . . ."

Garbish gave the other a look that was bright with malice. "Now, just why in the hell should you care, Frenchy?" he wanted to know. "It's the same beans and bacon and your hand out at the paymaster's table whether you're in the guardhouse at McKeogh or marchin' up the Fourth of July, ain't it? You got no beef."

Ladue shifted the tobacco in his cheek, his eyes spiteful with irritation. "Maybe I'm tired of beans and bacon and the McKeogh guardhouse," he said thinly. "Maybe tonight I go over the hill. Now, what do you think of that?"

Garbish shook his head disapprovingly. "You couldn't do that, Frenchy," he said. "Think of all them people in Sunbeam who are countin' on your hangin' to bring a little pleasure and light into their drab little lives. You wouldn't want to disappoint 'em by goin' over no hill."

"The hell I wouldn't," Ladue grunted. "And don't hold your breath until they tie a knot about my neck, you dumb son of a bitch. You'll be holdin' it for a long time if you do."

Garbish stretched and yawned and looked down the slope to where a little order was beginning to come out of the confusion now. He saw Quarterhill's big bay push through the willows toward where Ed Harvey was standing.

"I'll tell you something, Frenchy," he murmured. "I'll give

71

you some good advice. If I was you, I wouldn't make no try at goin' over the hill while I was takin' Quarterhill's orders. It could be damn' unhealthy."

"What you talkin' about?"

"The man's wore officer's rank in his time," Garbish said softly. "At least that's my guess. It is also my guess that if he thought it was the thing to do, he would have you stood up and shot and he would never bat an eyelid doin' it."

"Crap! What makes you think that?"

"Take a good look at his eyes sometime."

"I'll try to remember to," Ladue said sourly. "In the meantime, if I take a notion to go over the hill, I go."

"It's your funeral," Garbish said.

7

The March to Jensen's Ranch

Down on the flat Lieutenant Miller pressed a damp palm against the bark of an alder tree while he fought off the wave of pain that was running through him. It stabbed deep into his bowels and he knew, for he was a realistic man, that in all probability a Sioux bullet was about to put a period to the twenty years of service that belonged to First Lieutenant Jacob Bedwell Miller.

He'd been hit in the last seconds of the Sioux rush—just a thump like a heavy fist slamming into his side at first. It hadn't been until the last of the raiders had disappeared into the brush upriver that the pain had come as the anesthesia of shock had worn off. When it had hit he had turned and moved carefully toward the shade, afraid with each slow step that his legs might refuse to bear his weight any longer. Finally, braced against the tree, he'd explored the spreading dampness above his belt with methodical fingers. Not bleeding too much, but that could mean nothing, he decided. He could be bleeding to death inside.

He thought, making a vast effort to keep things marshaled strictly into line: *I have to stay on my feet until we get to Jensen's Ranch. Without an officer to lead it, this provisional troop will fall apart like a grain bag burst at the seams. . . . Colonel Howell will be at Jensen's. . . . Once I reach there I can turn the command of the troop over to him. . . .*

Another thought kept pushing at him, but he put it away, telling himself that he must concentrate on only one thing now—the business of getting back into the saddle somehow and of getting the troop on the march again. The minutes were ticking remorselessly away. There were so few of them left. . . .

The new thought, which he could not face, was that Jensen's Ranch lay between him and the Galena Reservation. And if the war party had hit here at Black Rock Crossing, had it not already struck at the ranch farther up the river? The idea that Jensen's might already be burned out—that Colonel Howell might already be dead—was too monstrous for Lieutenant Jacob Miller to entertain right now. He'd not think about it.

The pain stabbed again, driving a film of cold sweat out on Miller's forehead, and he waited until the pain had eased a little before he trusted his voice to call out to Ed Harvey. Harvey was a good man, but he was not strong enough to hold the troop together without an officer, Miller thought. It was better that Harvey knew no more than he had to know right now.

"Sergeant Harvey," he called then and hoped that his voice stayed flat and unrevealing. "Report here!"

Ed Harvey came up at a dogtrot, shame and disgust and solid temper showing in his red face as he hauled himself up and saluted. "Jailbirds, goldbricks, and no-goods!" he said violently. "Beggin' the lootenant's pardon, I'll have their goddamn' butts back in the saddle in a few minutes more. And the next time they will stand, by God, or—"

Miller cut him short, his voice reaching a little higher and becoming reedy as the pain stabbed again. "Never mind that now, sergeant. Get them mounted again and into a column of twos . . . We march for Jensen's Ranch at once. Send Private Riviera here with my horse . . . I will lead out."

A faint gnaw of worry suddenly erased the temper in Harvey's face as he looked more closely at Miller now. It wasn't like the lootenant to give an order that-a-way, he thought; the lootenant was a West Pointer and accustomed to giving orders according to the book. Harvey had always liked that.

"Sir," he said, the worry creeping into his voice as he stood straight in the hot sun, "is the lootenant feelin' all right? He looks kind of—"

Fresh pain turned Miller's voice razor-sharp. "Never mind about how I look, sergeant!" Now he remembered something else. He should have thought of it before, but things kept dancing around in his mind so. "Who was in command of that party on the slope . . . the ones who opened that flanking fire?"

"It had to be Lance Corporal Quarterhill, sir," Harvey answered as his worry began to put a cold lump into his belly now. "He must of sensed trouble—put his point up there on that knob instead of continuin' on, sir. He is a good man; I told the lootenant that this mornin', sir."

Too many words, Harvey knew sourly, but something was wrong here and the lootenant wasn't going to tell him, and so it was up to him to put a finger on what it was. Miller focused his attention on what Harvey was saying with an effort.

Quarterhill, he was thinking fuzzily. *Odd name. I have heard it before, but I do not remember where. It does not really matter, I suppose. All that matters is that we get to Jensen's Ranch . . . if there is a Jensen's Ranch . . .*

"Send him on to scout to Jensen's Ranch as fast as he can push his horses," Miller heard himself saying—too loudly, he thought. Much too loudly. He tried to keep his voice down as he dismissed Harvey. "That's all, sergeant."

Ed Harvey said, "Yes, sir," and rendered his salute and moved away, his seamed face thoughtful and unhappy. He was afraid that he had his answer. The lootenant wasn't fooling him any, he decided; he had seen too many men mortally hit in his time not to be able to read that fact in their faces. The lootenant had taken a bullet but was saying nothing about it.

And whether he said anything about it or whether he didn't, Ed Harvey was going to be the loser, Harvey knew glumly. Because, with the lootenant down, the command of Q Troop would settle onto Ed Harvey's shoulders, and that was something that he had no wish for. A first sergeant's job he could handle; an officer's job he could not. That thought sent a little thread of resentment running through him. God damn it, the lootenant getting knocked out this way was a dirty trick that he didn't deserve to have played on him! With effort he put the idea away.

Corporal Clendenning, sweat streaking the dust on his heavy jowls, was chewing out a recruit named Sells—wasting words and getting little done, Harvey saw with sour distaste as he caught up the reins of his mount and swung himself

75

into the saddle. He gave Clendenning an unfriendly stare and saw the dislike returned in the corporal's answering look.

"Go up to the knob and get Quarterhill," Harvey said curtly. "Tell him to report to me here."

Clendenning shrugged and pointed. "If you'd take trouble to use your eyes, you'd see he's already comin'," he said maliciously. "Gettin' old, Harvey?"

Harvey repressed the retort that was on the tip of his tongue as he saw Quarterhill's bay coming through the willows fifty yards upstream. He swung back to Clendenning.

"Get on about your business," he said heavily. He motioned at Trumpeter Riviera, holding Miller's horse and said, "Take the lootenant's mount to him, you. Ride with him as messenger. The rest of you heroes stand to horse!"

Webb Quarterhill walked his horse up, reined to a halt, and sat easily in the saddle, his face impassive, as Harvey rode over to meet him. Irascibility, mixed with worry, marked the sergeant major's craggy face, he noted.

"A point's job is out ahead of a column—not settin' on its asses on a hillside," Harvey snarled without preamble. "Did you know that, *Mister* Quarterhill?"

"I knew it," Webb said equably.

"Then what the hell were you doin' up there on that goddamn' knob?"

"Call it a hunch," Webb said.

The temper suddenly went out of Harvey. "And a hell of a good hunch it was," he said heavily. "If you had not been there Q Troop—if you can call it a troop—would be halfway back to Fort McKeogh by now. It is the Lootenant Miller's orders that you scout ahead to Jensen's Ranch, Lance Corporal Quarterhill. You are to get there as fast as your horses will take you."

"Right," Quarterhill said impassively.

"You will send back word of what you find there," Harvey concluded, his voice heavier still. "It is my thought that you will have no good news to send back. This expedition has had the curse of the devil on it from the start."

"Move out now, sergeant?"

"Move out now!"

Trumpeter Riviera, slim and careless—his handsome face

reflecting no concern behind its olive skin—got Jacob Miller's chunky gray. He checked the cinch and gathered up the reins to lead the horse toward the clump of alder where the lieutenant still stood, bracing himself with an arm on a tree.

"I brung the lootenant's horse, sir," Riviera said, halting a few paces away. "Sergeant Harvey said to . . ."

The trumpeter's voice trailed off and his eyes became startled and wary as he too saw the thing in Jacob Miller's face that Ed Harvey had seen. A vague grayness that the officer seemed to shed like an aura in the afternoon.

"Very good, soldier," Miller was saying in a voice that was too precise—too controlled, as if he was forming his lips carefully around each word. "Help me to mount, please. I think that I've got a small touch of sun . . ."

For a moment, as Riviera steadied the officer, he felt the other's dead weight come against him. Then Miller had both hands on the saddle and was hauling himself painfully up, got a leg across the horse's back. His unbuttoned blouse swung back momentarily so that the trumpeter caught a glimpse of the dark, moist patch that showed on Jacob Miller's shirt on the right side just above the top of his breeches.

Pain put red-hot spears into Miller now, and he fought off the wave of nausea that threatened to engulf him as he blindly found the stirrups with his feet. The dust flat, the willows, and the aspens—all shimmered in undulating waves before his eyes as he forced words through his lips.

"Follow me . . . I'll lead out . . ."

From a great distance he could hear Harvey's voice behind him. "Column of twos . . . walk . . . hoooooohh . . ."

The nausea had gone but a gray haze had come into the afternoon, Miller thought dully as he rode. Somehow he had to fight off that haze through the long, long hours that remained of this long, long day. A gray rider on a pale horse was back there following through that haze; he must not allow that rider to get close enough to touch his cold hand to Jacob Miller's shoulder until the column reached Jensen's Ranch. Because, with that cold touch, Jacob Miller would be no more . . .

Miller bit hard against his lower lip and forced his mind

77

to concentrate on the things that Colonel Felix Bexar had said to him the night before last. Or was it a million nights ago? Anyway, they were important things. Very important things . . .

"You will get to Ghost Basin before daylight on Saturday . . . I know that it is an impossible march. You must make it anyway, Jake. You must make it, anyway . . ."

He tried to keep the image of Colonel Felix Bexar in focus, but the colonel would not stay. He faded back into a maze of a hundred forgotten faces and now his mother's face occupied his mind instead. She was smiling reproachfully at him over the tops of her old-fashioned spectacles.

"Now, I must say that it took you long enough to come, Jacob," she was saying. "Well, that is the Army, I suppose. Anyway, welcome back to West Point . . ."

That was silly. This wasn't West Point. This was Wyoming Territory. There was no green plain here, no stately trees looking down on the Hudson as it rolled majestically out of the highlands. There was only sagebrush and lupine and Indian paintbrush and the cloud of brown dust, rising lazily into the still air, that the column made as it snaked its way along.

Miller turned a little in the saddle to look back, unheeding the sharper torment that the movement put into his body. He had to be sure, he thought. Yes, the gray rider was there, off on one flank of the troop, his gaunt face veiled by the brown fog of the dust. He was coming closer. . . .

Major Mark Faro had been thrown clear of the stage when it had rolled over, consciousness knocked out of him when his head had slammed onto the hard ground. That consciousness returned slowly to him now. He was aware that his mouth was parched and tasted bad. The sun seemed higher than it had a right to be and was shining into his face. His body was full of aches and pains . . . as if he had been flogged with a chain, he thought dully as he tried to remember what had happened.

It came back to him then. Those shots and yells. The wild flight of the stage and the panicky terror that had suddenly held him like a vise, shackling his brain and paralyzing his arms and legs. With a growing shame he remembered the scorn that had been in Lee Howell's eyes as she had seen him sitting there on the floor of the coach, waving his silly derringer.

"Oh, my God," he groaned aloud.

With an effort he managed to sit up. His fingers told him that there was dried blood on his face; at least he could move his arms and legs, he found with a swift relief. He rested there a little longer, conscious that the sun was becoming unpleasantly hot on his shoulders now. What did he do next, he wondered dully? The driver must be dead; the horses were gone. At any minute some of Hat's painted braves might come down this ravine looking for him. Lee must be somewhere about; he'd have to find her. . . .

A new thought came into Faro's mind with the suddenness of sunlight breaking through dark clouds. The cowhide case! How in hell had he forgotten that? Inside was the medicine that would drive the aches out of his body—chase the cobwebs from his brain and allow him to think surely again.

The wrecked stagecoach lay on its side a dozen yards away, and Faro crawled toward it on his hands and knees, not trusting himself to try and stand erect yet. He had seen Spiney put the bag in the boot in front of the driver's seat, he remembered. He reached the overturned vehicle at last, swearing petulantly at the sharp rocks which bit into his knees—then forgetting the pain as his clawing fingers reached for the leather apron of the boot. There were straps, and he fumbled at the buckles frantically.

A ghastly thought crept into his mind as he worked. Suppose that all the bottles had been broken in the crash? Or suppose that Spiney, guessing what the bag held, had not put it in the boot after all but had kept it for his own use? Those possibilities tortured Faro as he yanked more fiercely at the straps, sweat streaming down his dark face, leaving runnels in the dirt.

The last strap came loose; he pulled the apron aside, and his groping hands searched within. They touched something that felt like the thing he was searching for. He hauled it out with a violent wrench, saw that it was one of Lee Howell's bags, and flung it away with a curse. His search became more frantic; he was talking out loud but he didn't notice.

"It's got to be here! Oh, sweet Christ, it's got to be here! It's got to! It's got to!"

His fingers closed on a handle and he pulled a grip out, knowing that he couldn't stand it if he was disappointed again. Then he saw, with a great surge of elation, that it was the cowhide bag. He eased it to the ground and dragged it to where the stage made a small patch of shade. His fingers were shaking so badly now that he could hardly unfasten the straps; but it was done at last and his fingers touched the smooth, unbroken sides of the bottles that were nested in the lined pockets within.

He drew one of the bottles out, caressing its sleekness and admiring the shiny brown of the glass. With his teeth he worried the cork out—then tipped the bottle to his mouth and felt the restoring bite of the whiskey as it burned his throat.

Warmth began to come back into his belly and strength into his legs. "Ah, God," he said, and drank again.

After a little he recorked the bottle and slipped it into his pocket; then he carefully hid the bag in the safety of a thick clump of brush. He felt confident and sure of himself now. He was able to assess the situation with a cool mind.

He'd find Lee Howell and the two of them would go back to the ranch, keeping well away from the stage road, of course. Without mounts it was useless to think of trying to keep on for Doxy stage station. Jensen's was their best bet. Perhaps Howell and the rest had managed to beat off the Sioux attack. If so, well and good. If not, he and Lee could remain hidden in the hills above the ranch until the column arrived from Fort McKeogh.

Yes, that was the best plan. Utterly sound. Faro felt pleased with himself as he got to his feet. He'd show Lee Howell that he was quite capable of meeting a situation such as this. She'd be grateful—forget that she'd called him a coward.

Heavy sagebrush had partially broken Lee Howell's fall when she had been flung from the seat as the stage's front wheel had collapsed. Her head had hit hard against a root, knocking her out, but she had struggled back to consciousness now and was sitting up, propped by both hands, as Faro staggered toward her.

"Lee," he was calling. "Where are you? Are you all right, Lee? Answer if you can hear me."

A sudden reversal of feeling came over Lee as she called, "I'm here," and saw the swift relief light Faro's face as he came toward her. He had played a sorry part in the stage, but she could forgive that, she supposed; right now he was here and he was company in disaster. She wasn't wholly alone, and that was enough for now. He came on, blundering through the brush, to drop on one knee beside her as one of his arms went around her shoulders.

"Lee, are you all right?"

She tried a lopsided smile that increased Faro's feeling of protectiveness. A raw scratch marked one cheek and her face was smudged and dirty; her dress was torn and she had sage in her hair. Sudden remembrance came into her eyes.

"I'm still in one piece, I think," she said huskily. "I feel as if I had been through a rock crusher. . . . Help me up, Mark. What are we going to do now?"

Faro helped her to her feet and supported her with an arm around her waist. Without meaning to, Lee allowed her head to rest against his shoulder for a moment. She smelled the whiskey on his breath, but it didn't seem to matter. He was a soldier and he would know what to do. Right now, she didn't.

"We'll go back to the ranch," he was saying soberly. "It will be rough going because we must stay away from the stage road. Do you think that you can make it?"

"I can make it," Lee said, her voice suddenly turning hard. "I've got to make . . . Oh, God, I just remembered . . ."

For the first time that picture had come into her mind of Sam Howell on his knees in the dust in front of the ranch house while the painted riders ran toward him. The blood drained from Lee's face, leaving it gray beneath the dirt as she blindly turned away. Faro caught her and pulled her back to him.

"Here," he said harshly, lifting the bottle from his pocket. "Take a drink of this. It'll help."

He pushed the neck of the bottle against her teeth, and

in spite of her dislike for the taste of whiskey, Lee gulped twice. The liquor burned her throat and choked her but its warmth was comforting. After a moment the shaking in her legs stopped.

"I'm all right now," she said, pulling away from Faro's arm. "You are right . . . we must go back to the ranch."

It was brutal going as they kept to the hills above the bench. Faro went ahead, the canteen that he had taken from the stage slung from his shoulder and lugging the cowhide bag in his hand. Lee's eyes had been inquiring when he had started out with this awkward load. Faro's expression had told her nothing.

"Official papers," he said curtly. "Stuff that I can't afford to leave behind."

Their pace was snail slow as the sun crawled up the sky toward the zenith. There were sagebrush stretches that had to be covered carefully in case hostile eyes watched from the bench. There were rocky outcrops that had to be skirted and steep-sided ravines, choked with brush, which they clambered down into and climbed out of laboriously again. Sweat soaked their clothes and cut tracks through the dirt that streaked their faces.

They rested frequently, talking little. Once Lee said, "Perhaps they were able to drive the Sioux off at the ranch. They've been there before."

"We'll hope to God they did," Faro said.

"The troops should be here soon . . . if they can just hold out. Do you think they can?"

"We would hear the firing," Faro said heavily.

He saw the stricken look that came into Lee's eyes and wished that he'd held his tongue. Screened by the brush, he helped himself to the bottle again. It was the only friend he had, he thought blackly. The only thing he could trust.

They came finally to a hillside, dotted with firs, that looked down on the bench where the ranch lay in the early afternoon. Nothing stirred down there. Smoke still rose from the burned stable and the half-burned ranch house. In the cloudless sky three buzzards wheeled in slow circles.

"Oh, God," Lee said, her voice choked.

Faro's arm went about her. "Rest a little," he said, his voice trying to comfort her. "Then we will see what's to be done. I'll take care of everything, Lee."

The sun was dropping toward the western peaks, putting long shadows behind Webb Quarterhill and his five men as the trail, which had been climbing toward the hump of a low spur for the past quarter hour, now began to flatten again. Flanks and shoulders of the horses were darkly patched with sweat; in the bowl of the valley the day had been brutally hot. Quarterhill had pushed on as hard as he had dared; it would serve nothing to come to Jensen's Ranch with horses that were totally beat, he knew.

Off to one side the Sleepy Wind swung sharply to hug a rocky bluff and the ranch could not be far ahead, Quarterhill knew. He turned in his saddle as his horse breasted the last slope, and saw, far back, the yellow dust lifting in the last of the afternoon as it marked where Q Troop's column came on. The fact that they'd found no further sign of the war party that had hit the troop at the crossing meant nothing at all, Webb was thinking.

The beginnings of sunset were putting scarlet and gold fingers into the western sky, he saw as he swung to the front again. For the past hour his earlier forebodings had been weighing heavily on him as he rode. It was nothing that he could put a definite finger on; it was just a feeling that nothing was right in this day and that this march had been condemned to trouble and failure from the start. He tried to shake the thought away.

He could see now where a low bench, backed by the hills, narrowed the valley and ran parallel to the river. He wasn't sure but he thought that he could see a trace of smoke there in the coming sunset. Garbish pushed his horse up alongside, Ladue coming behind. Garbish had his long look.

"So," he said softly then. "I do not think that we are the only ones who have been visited by Hat's war parties today. That is Jensen's Ranch there on the bench."

"Jensen's," Ladue agreed in a curiously flat voice. He added with a quick, angry violence, "It's a damned good bet that there's little left there now."

8

Burial on the Bench

Quarterhill said nothing, but he knew that Ladue's prophesy had set bitter memories running in him. The country was different but he knew bleakly that he was riding toward the same sort of scene he had looked upon too often before. To ride up to the smoking ruins, the sad chimney monuments, of what had once been a home was something with which he had learned to live. It was not something he had learned to like.

Although he was not yet aware of it, Webb Quarterhill was gradually slipping back into the habits and the actions and the ways of thinking that had once belonged to Captain Quarterhill, C.S.A. The emotions stirring in him now were those that he had believed to be safely buried along his back trail.

He asked curtly, "Did Jensen have a family?"

Ladue nodded, his dark face expressionless once again. "A wife—two daughters. One was married to a man named Spiney. They all lived at the ranch with Old Man Jensen."

Quarterhill turned in his saddle and said curtly to young Clay Atkins, who had just ridden up, "Ride back to the column, son. Tell Lieutenant Miller that I think that Jensen's Ranch has been burned out. We're moving up to have a look. Say that I suggest that the lieutenant hold the troop behind this spur until I can get word back as to whether or not there are any Sioux ahead."

Atkins threw up a hand in acknowledgment, wheeled his horse, and sent it back down the steep track at a run. Quarterhill swung back again to the others, and the faintly sardonic amusement in Mitch Garbish's eyes suddenly reminded him that it was hardly customary for brand-new lance corporals to advise their troop commanders on the tactics that they should use. Ladue and the others had walked their horses a little way down the side of the spur so that Garbish's easy spoken words reached Quarterhill's ears alone as the two sat in their saddles.

"Now and then," Garbish murmured, "it comes to me that I can see more than a noncom's stripes on you, friend Quarterhill. You wouldn't have ridden at the head of your own troop at one time, would you now? It seems to fit."

The stare that Quarterhill gave back was flat and hard. "Keep your guessing to yourself, Mitch," he said softly. "A man can get into trouble by guessing out loud too much."

Garbish returned the stare, his look placid and undisturbed. "Give it no more thought, Reb," he said without rancor. "Just put me down as bein' the nosy kind. Well, do we get about scoutin' that cottonwood flat down there?"

Quarterhill nodded with a hard jerk of his head and kneed his horse on to where the rest of the squad waited. "Mitch, you and Hess scout along the flats by the river—watch for sign that would indicate that the Sioux are heading for Fourth of July Creek. Jones and Dolliver, follow the edge of the hills until we get to the bench. Ladue and I will keep to the trail. If nobody's got any questions we'll move out."

There were no questions and he led the way down until they reached the cottonwood flats; then he swung his arm and the two sets of flankers broke away to right and left at a trot, the trees swallowing them before they had gone a hundred yards. Quarterhill gave them ten minutes to get their distances, then lifted his own tired mount into a trot as Ladue spurred up to ride on his left. The two of them spoke only once as they moved through the dappled shade streaked by the last of the sunlight.

"That was smoke above the bench," Ladue said with a curious, intense harshness in his voice. "By now Hat will have finished with his scalping and burning at Jensen's and will be gone into the hills—most likely up the Fourth of July. So what do we do? Let the son of a bitch go unpunished?"

"We do not," said Quarterhill, the harshness in his own voice matching that in Ladue's. "We go after him."

Ladue looked at Quarterhill out of the corners of his eyes.

85

"I wonder," he said sourly. "I saw the lootenant before we left the crossing. He's been hit—hit bad. Who's goin' to take his place? Ed Harvey? I don't think so."

"Why not?" Quarterhill asked roughly.

Again Ladue gave him that oblique look. "Harvey's a good man," he said, half as if he spoke to himself. "He ain't good enough to take this half-assed troop up the Fourth of July after Hat. We'll bury the Jensens and go home."

"Like hell we will!"

The conversation died, and again Quarterhill felt a faint derision that he should be saying what Q Troop would or would not do. He tried to recapture his earlier detachment—his indifference to the march of events. He couldn't do it. Somehow the smoke that he'd seen there above the bench had turned this expedition into something that was personally important to him.

He moved his shoulders impatiently as he shook the confused thoughts away. He had plenty of immediate chores, he decided. To hell with the rest of it.

The trees began to thin, gave way presently to sagebrush, and Quarterhill had his first near look at the bench that ran its long tongue down into the flat half a mile ahead. The ruined buildings of Jensen's Ranch, that smoke haze still hanging over them, were still another half a mile farther on,. where the bench flattened against fir-covered hills. Along the narrowing valley between bench and river he could see the cleft, already deep in shadow, where the canyon of the Fourth of July drove back into the high and broken ground on the far side of the Sleepy Wind.

The trail began its gentle climb up the bench's nose, and Quarterhill and Ladue rode in silence until they emerged from the willows of a little draw and Jensen's lay a hundred yards in front of them. With a common accord they reined in and sat for a moment, still saying nothing as they looked.

There was a pole corral, empty of stock and with two of its sections torn down; to one side, still smoldering in the last of the day, was a burned barn. A wagon shed, with a light wagon beneath it, had been left unburned, as had been what looked to be a blacksmith shop. Nearer at hand a part of the ranch house still stood, smoke leaking out through its smashed windows. The main part of the building was in ashes, but the log walls of the kitchen part still remained. There were no signs of life.

Quarterhill sat in his saddle, looking for a long moment. The expression on his dark face was withdrawn and marked with a faint regret. A buzzard wheeled high in the evening sky on motionless wings; a jay scolded from a pine, and a camp robber put its mournful plaint into the lengthening shadows. As Quarterhill had expected, a blackened chimney stood amid the ruins to mark the place where Old Man Jensen, his wife, and his two daughters and his son-in-law had once lived. . . .

Another of those grim monuments.

Ladue's voice broke into Quarterhill's dark thoughts. "Mitch and Hess ridin' in from the river," he said, that stillness again in his saturnine face.

Quarterhill nodded and waited for the two to thread their way through the willows of the gully and emerge onto the bench again. Garbish's eyes flickered briefly across the smoking ruins that lay ahead, then returned to Quarterhill as he grunted noncommittally and eased his big frame in the saddle.

"We cut Indian trail," he reported. "Headed for the Fourth of July, all right. About the same size war party as the one that hit us at the crossing. My guess is that it's the same one. You see any sign of the Jensens yet?"

Quarterhill shook his head. "We just got here," he said. "Come on—we'll look now."

"I don't figure they'll be hard to find," Garbish grunted, with no expression in his voice as he moved his horse up to ride beside Quarterhill. He tipped his head a little to glance at the buzzard circling in the sky. "That trail was pretty fresh—not more'n a couple of hours old. From the looks of things they must of hit this place early this mornin'—then come on down the river and run into us, Reb."

"Yes," Quarterhill said shortly.

He pushed his horse along the bench, the animal quivering and uneasy as they passed the nearest of the burned buildings. Samp Dolliver and Amen Jones were climbing the bench from the left now, Quarterhill noted absently; from the easy way they sat in the saddle, not pushing their mounts, he guessed that they had found no sign of the Sioux on the far side of the valley. That meant that Hat's main band had already headed up the Fourth of July on its way to the big powwow in Ghost Basin, he guessed.

The two flankers saw them now and came on at a trot. Now Hess, the hare-lipped trooper, hauled his mount up short a dozen yards away and sat looking. He said in a thick voice, his words carrying, "God damn all Injuns to hell!" His deformed mouth gave his words an odd violence.

Quarterhill, his three with him, rounded the partly burned ranch house, where the scene of the attack was laid out before them. Not pretty. It told a mute story.

Old Man Jensen, scalped and mutilated, lay face down in a clump of sagebrush. Near the stage road a heavy-set man in a bloodstained blue uniform was sprawled in the dust, arms flung out and his head crushed. He'd gone down fighting, for empty cartridge brass was scattered about him. Farther on, by the corral, was a third man pincushioned with Sioux arrows.

"Colonel Howell and Grimes, the Indian agent," Garbish said softly. "Hat and his braves must of hated Grimes's guts for what they done to him, Reb."

"Spread out and look for the women and the son-in-law," Quarterhill said harshly. "Garbish and I will go through the house. Sing out if you find anything."

He dismounted heavily and tied his horse to the corral, then went back toward the house on foot, Garbish following behind. A new thought had struck Quarterhill, putting a sharp thread of worry into him. The stage from Sunbeam, with Lee Howell on it, should have stopped here yesterday for the night. It wasn't here now. Had it gone on this morning and been hit by the same war party farther up the river? A cold feeling hit Quarterhill in the belly as he knew that was almost a certainty if the stage *had* gone on.

The thought of Lee Howell in the hands of Hat's red murderers made him want to retch. With an effort he forced himself to think coldly and logically of this thing. Colonel Howell, dead there in the road, must have been here when the stage arrived yesterday. He'd not have let it continue on toward Galena knowing what he then knew; he would have sent it back to Sunbeam either last night or early this morning. It had to be that way, he decided as he came to the house and moved around it.

The stink of smoke was almost overpowering as he and Garbish entered the unburned wing. The inside was a shambles made up of furniture overturned and broken, the floor littered with smashed crockery, torn clothing, and dumped food. They found what was left of Spiney, his body half burned, lying in a doorway that opened onto the ashes of the rest of the house. They had carried him outside and laid him down beside the wall when Amen Jones called from where a shallow draw ran down to the river.

The women were there, the three of them lying like bundles of torn and soiled clothing in the spots where they had been flung. Mercifully they were dead. Hess made sick, retching sounds as he turned away. Anger became a cold and steadying thing in Quarterhill as he swung around to Garbish.

"Take them up by the house—then see if you can find shovels in the blacksmith shop," he said harshly. "Get working on a grave. Ladue, ride back to the troop. Tell Lieutenant Miller what we've found here. Tell him that the indications are that the Sioux have headed up Fourth of July canyon."

Ladue was sitting motionless on his horse, hands quiet on the saddle in front of him while he looked down into the little draw with eyes that seemed to have retreated more deeply into the dark mask of his face. Quarterhill repeated the order, his voice rising in a sharper note. Ladue stirred.

"Send somebody else, Quarterhill," the trooper said thinly. "I used to know the younger girl; Old Man Jensen would bring her to Sunbeam once in a while. I guess she'd sort of like to have a friend here when she's buried."

Quarterhill looked sharply at the other; then he nodded in sober agreement as he nudged his horse forward. He was about to send Dolliver with the message when he saw that two riders had broken out of the cottonwoods across the flat and were coming on, riding hard. Even at that distance he recognized who they were. Young Atkins and Ed Harvey. Something had happened back there at the column to make an old soldier like Harvey push tired mounts that way, Quarterhill knew as he rode to meet them.

89

Harvey reined up, making no attempt to hide the worry in his face as his eyes went on beyond Quarterhill to the ruins of the ranch on the bench. Atkins hesitated awkwardly for a moment; then he rode on toward where Garbish and Amen Jones were coming from the blacksmith shop with shovels in their hands. Harvey let his breath run out with a whistling tiredness.

"They all dead?" he asked heavily.

Quarterhill nodded his sober confirmation. "All of them, Ed," he said harshly. "They must have been surprised—the men were all scattered. We found the three women dead and violated in a dry gulch in back of the house."

Harvey rocked his head with a sharp impatience. "What about Colonel Howell and Grimes, the Indian agent? My God, they're not dead too, are they?"

"Dead too," Quarterhill said in that same flat voice. "Grimes was by the corral, shot full of arrows. Colonel Howell was in the road, his head smashed with a war club."

Harvey's face settled into deep lines that showed all of his years. "I am sorry," he said. "Howell was a good man. . . . I am even more sorry for the troop."

"Why the troop?"

Harvey made no answer to that at once as a thoughtful look suddenly relieved the bleakness of his face a little. "That Major Faro," he said. "He should have been here on the stage last night, Lance Corporal Quarterhill. He is not dead?"

"If he is, we haven't found him," Quarterhill said, his voice turning hard at the mention of Faro's name. "There's no sign of the stage here that we've seen."

"By God, we've got to find him!"

"Why?"

Harvey gave Quarterhill a dour look out of the corners of his eyes. "Because, if we don't find him pretty soon, the provisional troop is goin' to be all out of officers, is why," he said, and his words reminded Webb of how Lieutenant Miller had looked in the brief moment that he'd seen him, standing in the shade of the alders back there at the crossing.

He remembered, too, what Ladue had said earlier. He had given it little thought at the time—put it down to an old soldier's habitual griping about things.

"Miller's been hit?" he asked sharply.

Harvey's nod was glum. "I should of seen it before," he said in a voice that was a little defensive. "I was ridin' at the tail of the column, though, to keep them misfits we got from stragglin' all of the way back to McKeogh. The lootenant fell out of his saddle when we halted back there behind the spur."

"How bad is he?" Quarterhill asked thinly. "His wound can't be too bad if he's been able to ride for better than three hours from the crossing, Ed."

"It's bad," Harvey said. "How he stuck in the saddle as long as he did is something I do not know. He took a bullet in the belly and it's still in him. . . . I have got to find this Major Faro and find him fast. He can take over command of the troop until we get back to Fort McKeogh. . . ."

Ed Harvey allowed his voice to trail raggedly away, and he failed to meet Quarterhill's eyes as understanding suddenly came into them. It made a lot of things plain that hadn't been plain before. Now he didn't like what he knew.

Ed's afraid that he'll be left in command of the troop, he thought sardonically; then he eased his judgment a little as his mind ran on. *Maybe I don't blame him, at that—this whole business has been screwed up from the start. Maybe I wouldn't be too happy, myself, if I had the responsibility for Q Troop from here on in, because things are going to get worse. Not better.*

Harvey was going on, his voice a little more assured now. "Clendenning's bringin' the troop on up here. . . . I told him to rig up a horse litter for the lootenant while I come on ahead to find Colonel Howell. Well, Major Faro will do, I guess."

He kneed his horse on toward the ranch buildings, Quarterhill riding beside him. "My God, Ed," he said savagely, "try to think a little clearly, will you? There's no Faro here. The chances are a hundred to one that he's dead too. Either that or the stage is almost back to Doxy by now. If the lieutenant dies, you're in charge of the troop and you can't change that!"

He'd push it hard at Harvey, Quarterhill decided grimly. If Jacob Miller died, the provisional troop would disintegrate like salt poured into a bucket of water unless somebody rode those thirty-odd men with a tight rein and a rough spur. They were held together by no special bonds of discipline or loyalty; only a strong man could hold them to the task that had to be done. And right now, Ed Harvey was the only strong man in sight.

Harvey read some of that thought into Quarterhill's harsh speech, for he turned and looked at the younger man now with bitter and angry eyes. He too knew what had to be done. Better than Quarterhill, he knew that he did not possess the capacity to do it. It was not something that he had contracted for when he had held up his hand and taken the oath, he thought sourly.

"The lootenant ain't dead yet, Lance Corporal Quarterhill," he said in a heavy voice. "And I do not need advice from you; I will find this Faro if I have to look behind every bush between this place and . . ." His words trailed off morosely.

The two of them came around the corner of the half-burned ranch house, and Quarterhill reined up suddenly, swearing under his breath. "It may be that you've found him at that, Ed," he said softly. "And Miss Howell with him."

He could see the pine-studded slopes of the hills that climbed from behind the wagon shed and the blacksmith shop now. Two people had come into view some three hundred yards away and were moving downhill toward the bench. Too far to see their faces, but Quarterhill knew that the slender man in the uniform had to be Mark Faro; the woman with him had to be Lee Howell.

It was curious how the wheels turned, Quarterhill was thinking with a vague detachment as he turned his horse toward the slope. The man who had dishonored his parole was now about to take command of Q Troop; the man to whom he had given that parole would now be taking his orders. Quarterhill had not the slightest doubt as to how this thing would finally end.

Faro waved his arms now and broke into a clumsy run, leaving the girl behind. He was still two hundred yards away when he stumbled and fell. He lay there on his face for a moment; then he got back to his feet and stood, brushing the dirt from his uniform, as Lee Howell passed him, her face averted.

The man's either wounded or drunk, Quarterhill thought, a little puzzled. *If he's wounded, I wonder that Lee doesn't stop for him. Well, none of my business.*

It didn't occur to him that it was odd to think of her as "Lee," not as "Miss Howell," as he dismounted now and began to climb the slope toward her. She wore the same gray dress that she had worn on the train, he noted. It was badly torn and smeared with dirt. Dirt smudged her face and the dried blood from a nasty scratch marked one cheek. From the corners of his eyes he saw that Mark Faro had changed his course down the slope and that Ed Harvey was hurrying to meet him. As the sergeant approached the officer's bearing changed to an arrogant casualness, which contrasted oddly with the way he had come out of the timber.

"Miss Howell, ma'am," Webb said, reaching a hand to steady Lee as she almost fell into his arms. "I'm Private Quarterhill. . . . we met briefly on the train."

"Thank you," she said in a low voice, and Quarterhill knew that she was fighting hard to control herself. "What has happened? Is my father all right?"

"I am sorry," Quarterhill said soberly, and he wished that he knew of some way to make this easier. There was no way, he knew, but he held her a little more firmly as he said, "Colonel Howell is dead."

He saw the stricken look that came into her eyes, and she clung to him hard for a moment. Presently she gained control, and disengaging herself gently, she stood proud and straight. Her voice was almost steady as she said, "Take me to him, please, Private Quarterhill. I knew it had to be so."

The last of the sunset washed across the bench, lending a softness to the pines that ringed the spot where the shallow graves had been prepared. Quarterhill spoke softly, and he and his six troopers uncovered. Then Amen Jones moved forward with his worn Bible in his hand. He waited as Quarterhill lifted Lee Howell to her feet from where she had been kneeling; then he began to read softly from the Gospel according to St. Luke.

"*. . . for they are equal unto the angels . . . and they*

are the children of God . . . being the children of the resurrection . . . amen. . . ."

A camp robber put his plaint into the evening as Amen Jones closed the book. Mitch Garbish and Samp Dolliver took up the shovels again to do what was to be done. . . . Ladue, his dark face expressionless, stood for a moment watching—then moved off into the coming night. Quarterhill touched Lee's elbow.

"I am sorry," he said.

Already his mind had moved on to other things. *I'd better set an outpost before it gets too dark,* he was thinking. *Harvey will be tied up with Faro and may not think of it. And unless I am very badly mistaken, it will not be long before I will be facing a showdown with Major Mark Faro.*

He waited for Lee Howell's answer, but she was already moving away toward where Provisional Q Troop was going into bivouac beneath the cottonwoods on the bench. That was just as well, Quarterhill knew. He possessed small talent for comforting words. Faro would be better at that.

9

Bargain in the Wagon Shed

The whiskey was dying out in Major Mark Faro and he needed another drink badly now. That funeral in the last of the sunset had shaken him badly—more than he cared to admit—and it had been made worse by the fact that Jacob Miller was badly wounded, probably dying, on the pallet that had been fixed for him in the blacksmith shop. The knowledge that he was now in command of this ragtag troop did nothing to soothe Faro's jangling nerves.

He'd been a fool to cache that cowhide bag, with his whiskey in it, up there on the hillside, he decided morosely. Thank God it was almost dark now. In a few minutes he could slip away and bring that bag down here and hide it nearer at hand in a safe place. After that, he'd be able to think clearly—decide what he must do. Return to Fort McKeogh, he thought. He had no intention of leading this rabble up Fourth of July canyon; that much he knew. Old Bexar could lump it if he didn't like it.

A tight little knot of riders headed down the bench in the shadows, and Faro heard a man's voice sing out. He started a little. He'd not forget that voice, he knew grimly; it belonged to Quarterhill. Somehow he'd manage to get rid of the fellow before they got back to the fort, but that too could wait at the moment. He started, nerves jangling again, as a voice spoke behind him.

"Beggin' the major's pardon, sir."

Faro turned, his dark face twisted and lips pulled back from his teeth as he saw that it was Harvey, the acting first sergeant, standing there respectfully. Then the major relaxed a little. This was an old soldier; he could handle his kind.

"What is it, sergeant?" he asked coldly.

"Sir, the Lootenant Miller is pretty bad," Harvey said, choosing his words carefully. His relief at finding Faro alive was beginning to be tempered a little by a growing distrust now—Harvey wasn't quite sure why. "Would the major look at him?"

"What good will looking at him do?"

The words increased Harvey's uneasiness. The tone was not that of a soldier, Harvey thought; rather, it was the tone of a man who was nearing the breaking point, and that was not good. It meant that the weight of command was likely to be riding Ed Harvey's shoulders again, and he didn't like that.

"Sir," he said carefully, "maybe, if you could get the bullet out of the lootenant——"

"God damn it, sergeant, I'm not a doctor!" Faro snapped, and he knew that he had gone too far as he saw the expression that came into the noncom's face in the fading light. He eased his tone as he went on. "Sorry, sergeant. I guess my nerves are a little on edge. I'll see to Lieutenant Miller presently. I've got a couple of other things I must do first."

"Yes, sir," Harvey said, his face stolid now. "Sorry to have bothered the major."

"All right. All right."

Harvey started to turn away—stopped and swung back, his mouth set stubbornly now. "Sir, if the major don't mind a suggestion. We better march again not later than midnight if we are goin' to get to Ghost Basin in time."

Faro's overtaut nerves snapped. "God damn it, sergeant," he said, a wild note creeping into his voice, "I don't need *you* to tell me my business! And, for your information, we're not marching to Ghost Basin; we're marching back to McKeogh!"

For a long moment Ed Harvey stood, staring back at Faro in the last of the daylight. Then he lifted his hand in his precise salute and swung on his heel.

"Yes, sir," he said.

Faro watched as Harvey disappeared in the gloom, his lips set petulantly as little tremors ran through him. This was too much, by God! A wounded lieutenant and an old fool of a sergeant and that son of a bitch Quarterhill on his trail! Well, they'd go back to Fort McKeogh just the same,

96

and if old Bexar tried to make anything of it, he'd report to Washington that the colonel had sent a totally inadequate force out after Hat. General Romney would be glad enough to believe that; he was after Bexar's scalp, anyway. Faro's skirts would be clean.

It was dark enough now to go after that bag. Once he had it, he'd be able to handle these things, he had no doubt. He suited the thought to the action and started along the bench. Once clear of the ranch, he broke into a run.

Corporal Clendenning, who had a nose for such things, had overheard the conversation between Harvey and Faro from the little clump of brush where he had stood concealed. A look of heavy satisfaction spread over the corporal's face now. Things were breaking very nicely, he considered. He had no stomach for marching up the Fourth of July after Hat, and he thought that he had just found a way to be sure that he didn't.

The major's half-incoherent conversation had confirmed what Clendenning had suspected earlier. The man was a drunk. Likely he had liquor hidden around somewhere. Clendenning had smelled the whiskey on Faro's breath earlier, and he had not missed those signs that betray a man when the drink is dying out in him. Well, he'd just make sure that he got his hands on that hootch . . . Faro would be his man then.

He started along the bench in cautious pursuit.

It was full dark now as Faro scrambled up the slope, falling often, getting up and going on as the frenzy built up in him. Suppose he couldn't find the spot where he had hidden the bag? Suppose some stray Indian, who had stayed behind, had found it and carried it away? The imaginings were almost more than Faro could bear and he tried to force his tortured mind away from them, but they kept returning.

He had to find that bag! The thought of the warming whiskey in those dark bottles tortured him. He could feel the bite of that whiskey in his throat, and thinking of that put cold sweat into the palms of his hands.

A dozen times he thought that he had found the spot; a dozen times he almost wept as he found that he was wrong. He needed light but he didn't dare try to make a torch;

that would give his secret away to those who were camped below. They'd want some of his whiskey. He couldn't bear the thought.

A full moon began to edge up presently beyond the rim of the mountains to the east and its faint light helped a little. Faro finally spotted the scarred pine that marked the rock where he had hidden the bag, and his relief was so great that tears started down his face. He scrambled toward it on all fours, clawed desperately at the pine needles that he had earlier raked over the bag. It was there! His fingers touched the cowhide.

"Ah, God!" he said aloud.

He got the cork out of a bottle and drank, the liquor slobbering down over his chin, and now life began to come back into him again. He hunched himself until his back was against the tree as he caressed the bottle with his hands and felt a deep peace begin to descend on him. He drank again. . . .

A long time later—just how long he didn't know and didn't care—Major Mark Faro started back down the slope once more. The moon was well up now, shedding an eerie and uncertain light over the bench where the ravaged ranch stood and Provisional Q Troop was camped beneath the cottonwoods. As he reached the level ground, Faro stopped and carefully put the bag down while he brushed off his uniform and set his hat at a jaunty angle, picked the bag up, and went on, his step springy.

He felt capable—sure of himself now. He'd take things over here at Jensen's Ranch; he'd get everything organized tonight, and then they would start back for Fort McKeogh tomorrow. A new thought entered his mind, further justifying his decision. There was that wounded lieutenant—what was his name? Miller? And there was a woman—Lee Howell. It was his duty to see that they got back to safety. That alone was excuse enough for not leading this rabble on a wild goose chase up the Fourth of July.

A certain smugness crept into him as he thought of Lee Howell now. She was a damned beautiful woman, and a damned desirable one too. After she got over the shock and grief of her father's death she would be grateful to Mark Faro for getting her safely out of this. The thought filled Faro with a warm satisfaction. He had a way with women, he told himself.

He went on, keeping to the shadows and staying well away from the campfires that glowed beneath the cottonwoods. The murmur of men's voices came faintly to him, but he did not try to make out the words. His first concern was to get the bag hidden in a safe place; he wanted no more hell such as he had gone through this evening. The weight in his hand made him feel safe and secure as he quickened his pace.

He had almost reached the shelter of the wagon shed when he saw a figure detach itself from the shadows by the blacksmith shop fifty feet away and move out into the moonlight. Then he recognized the square set of Ed Harvey's shoulders and swore under his breath. A second figure joined Harvey, and their voices carried to Faro as he dodged into the deeper gloom of the shed.

"Where's that damned major?" Harvey was asking in his gravelly voice. "He said he'd be here."

"I been through the camp; he ain't there, sarge," the other voice said. "I been through it twice."

"Then go through it a third time," Harvey said sourly, lifting his voice a little. "If you can't find him, send Quarterhill here. I can't take care of the lootenant by myself!"

"Quarterhill ain't come back from postin' the outpost detail yet, sarge."

"Send him as soon as he comes! Jesus, have I got to tell you everything, Wheelding?"

Harvey swung back into the shadows of the blacksmith shop and Faro saw Trooper Wheelding start toward the wagon shed. *He mustn't find me here with the bag*, Faro thought with sudden panic. *I'll hide it here temporarily—come back for it later.* He felt his way through the gloom, stumbling over harness, which had been scattered by the Indians, and found the light wagon he had seen there earlier. There was a pile of canvas under the seat; he thrust the bag beneath it and made sure it was covered.

Moving quietly now, he skirted the end of the shed and stepped out into the moonlight just as Wheelding came up. The trooper stopped abruptly, relief showing on his face in the moonlight as he saluted clumsily.

"Sir," he said, "Harvey—I mean Sergeant Harvey—wants to see the major in the blacksmith shop right away. It's about Lootenant Miller, sir."

"Very good, soldier," Faro said brusquely. "I was on my way there—lead on!"

It was a littered room and not large. A smoking and smelly lantern hung from a wire above the forge; Lieutenant Jacob Miller, his face white beneath the dark stubble of his beard, lay on a rude pallet beside the anvil block. Ed Harvey knelt beside him, a canteen in his hand. Harvey looked up, his eyes turning wary as he saw Faro in the doorway.

"How is he?" Faro asked.

"Bad, sir. Unconscious again."

Faro moved on into the lantern light, avoiding looking at Miller after his first glance. There were dark stains on the pallet, and the sight of blood had always unnerved him. He turned to look back out into the moonlit night.

"That confirms my decision," he said, making his words curt and incisive. "We march for Fort McKeogh at daybreak, sergeant. We must get this man to a doctor."

"Sir, our mission is——"

"Never mind the mission, sergeant," Faro said, his voice sharpening. "I am in command here now. Just see to it that this troop—if you can call it that—is ready to march tomorrow morning. Is that quite clear?"

Ed Harvey stayed on one knee, looking up and with no expression showing in his red, craggy face. For the space of half a dozen breaths he didn't answer; when he finally did speak, his voice was like a dry and rustling wind.

"Yes, sir. It's clear."

Faro wheeled out into the night again, almost bumping into Lee Howell as he did so. He put out a hand to touch her arm, saw her draw abruptly away from him.

"Lee," he said, "I didn't see——"

"I heard what you just said to Sergeant Harvey, major," she answered, her voice cold and withdrawn. "I assume that you were not serious; the mission of this troop is to go after Hat. I thought my father made that quite clear last night."

"But Lee—Miss Howell," Faro said, his voice a little flustered—"the situation was quite different then. Don't you see? Now, Lieutenant Miller's been badly wounded—you're here! I have to get both of you back to Fort McKeogh. We can worry about Hat and his Indians after that."

"You needn't worry about me, major," Lee said coldly. "As for Lieutenant Miller, he's a soldier. If he could give the orders, he would say go on!"

"There's no need for it! What possible difference can a few days make?"

"The difference between a hundred people dying in addition to those who died here today, major," Lee told him. "Let me pass, please. I must do what I can for Lieutenant Miller."

Faro stared after her, his decision wavering for a moment. He had not missed that implication that Miller was a soldier and he was not, and for a moment it roweled his pride. Then he remembered the dark mouth of the canyon of the Fourth of July, as he had seen it in the dying light of the afternoon, and he thought of the screaming warriors charging out of the willows this morning, and Mark Faro knew that he was not going after Hat. Some of the arrogance came back into him as he walked away.

He remembered that bag in the wagon shed and decided that he must move it to a safer place. Better not approach the shed from the blacksmith shop, though. He would swing around by the bivouac just in case that trooper Wheelding should be watching. No need to take chances now. It was a long two days back to Fort McKeogh.

His pace was deliberate as he neared the cottonwoods. Through a thin screen of low brush he could see the glow of the fires where troopers boiled coffee and fried bacon and talked in subdued voices. He could make out the words now, and Faro paused to listen as a man's voice, higher than the rest, carried across the mottled light beneath the trees.

"I tell you I ain't ridin' up no Fourth of July Creek," the voice said with angry emphasis. "God damn it, the lootenant's dying—Wheelding told me so! So who's goin' to say what we do? Old Harvey? Well, the hell with him! I ain't takin' orders to ride up that goddamn' creek from no sergeant!"

"What about that fancy major?" another voice asked.

"All right, what about him?" the first man demanded, his tone more truculent. "Clendenning says he ain't nothin' but a goddamn' staff son of a bitch out of Washington. What the hell right has *he* got to give us orders?"

"Maybe he don't want to go up Fourth of July Creek no more'n we do, Henny. Ever think of that?"

"Then him an' me'll get along fine."

"Aw, take it easy," a third voice said. "Everything's goin' to be okay. Clendenning said so."

"And what the hell does Clendenning know about it, Tash? That fat bastard don't know nothin'!"

"That's what you think, Henny. Corporal Clendenning's a fixer. He'll bring that snotty major into line."

Faro swung away, heading for the wagon shed again. He'd teach this rabble a lesson before they ever got back to Fort McKeogh, he decided as a vicious anger ran through him. He'd burn their asses for them; he'd make them wish that they had never been born, by God! As for that smart bastard, Clendenning—whoever *he* was—he'd send *him* off on a scout into hostile territory along with Quarterhill. That would take care of both of them!

He came up to the shadows of the wagon shed and stood listening for a moment. No sound reached him except the mutter of men's voices beneath the trees. Faro stepped into the darkness of the shed and confidently groped his way toward the wagon. Everything was as he had left it, he concluded, as he thrust a hand beneath the canvas. Then a sudden nausea gripped his throat.

The bag was no longer there!

He scrambled up into the bed of the wagon and searched more frantically. Maybe he had remembered wrong. Maybe he'd left the bag in the back instead of the front of the wagon. It was another full minute before he had to admit despairingly to himself that the bag, with its precious cargo, was no longer there. He held his head and fought the sickness that was in him.

"Oh, my God," he said aloud.

Corporal Clendenning stepped out of the deep shadow where he had been hidden. He had been waiting for the major to come. The deep despair that had been in the major's voice had told Clendenning that he had been right in his guess about this man.

"Lose something, major?" he asked slyly now.

A sudden hope started in Faro. "My medicine," he said. "It was in a cowhide bag. Have you seen it, soldier?"

"Well, now," Clendenning said, grinning to himself in the darkness, "I guess I must of thought that old cowhide bag was something somebody had throwed away, major."

"What have you done with it?" Faro's voice rose higher. "Return it to me at once! Do you hear?"

"I hear." Clendenning's chuckle was almost audible. "Let's talk about it a little first, major. I figure that bag is pretty valuable. You wouldn't want it to get lost."

"Damn your insolence! Give me that bag immediately! I'll put you under arrest if you don't!"

This time Clendenning's amusement was audible. "Now, major, you wouldn't want to do that," he said. "We're 'way out here in the sticks where they don't dispense none of your kind of medicine, see? If you was to get mean with me like that, most likely that bag of yours would get lost permanent. You wouldn't want that."

Things were working out nicely, Clendenning was thinking. He'd judged his man correctly. This major, for all his fancy manners, wasn't going to risk being stranded out here without his whiskey, he knew. And he'd be safe even after they got back to McKeogh because he knew this man's secret and it was one that Faro would pay him to keep, unless he was badly mistaken. There should be money and promotion in it for Corporal Clendenning.

The arrogance had gone out of Faro's voice as he answered. "Just get me the bag, whoever you are," he said.

"The name's Clendenning," the corporal grunted. "And don't you worry none about that medicine of yours, major. I'll see that you get a little of it when you need it, see? We'll both have a little of it; it'll be good for us."

"Give it to me now!"

"Easy, easy. We ain't done talkin' yet," Clendenning said, coming out of the deeper shadows. "Now, the boys ain't too damn' happy about this fool march up the Fourth of July. Maybe you ought to say how *you* feel about it."

103

"We're going back to Fort McKeogh," Faro said sullenly. "We're not going up the Fourth of July."

"Well, now, that makes everything mighty nice, major," Clendenning said with satisfaction. "The boys'll be right happy to hear that. Yes, sir, they will."

"My medicine," Faro said hoarsely. "I've got to have it! Get it for me now, damn you!"

"I told the major i'd take care of it," Clendenning said blandly. "I got a little whiskey along with me, though. We could share a nip of that. It might help the major's belly."

10

Soldier and Surgeon

Moonlight lay in a soft wash across the bench as Quarterhill came back from posting his outguards. Garbish and Dolliver watching the canyon of the Fourth of July, Clay Atkins and Hess downriver, Ladue and Amen Jones at the edge of the hills to the southwest. He'd send others out to relieve them in due time, Quarterhill thought as he dismounted by the corral.

The enclosure had been repaired, he noted absently as he paused to load tobacco into his pipe. The troop horses milled inside, and he scowled in the moonlight, wondering if Ed Harvey had been out of his mind to order that. Or had it been Faro? If Q Troop should be jumped in the dark, the troopers would play hell trying to catch loose, frightened mounts. He'd suggest to Harvey that he'd better stretch a picket line.

Cooking fires made a red glow under the cottonwoods a hundred yards away across the bench, and the faint smell of coffee reminded Quarterhill that he hadn't eaten since morning and that he was hungry. He turned in that direction, expecting that he'd find Harvey there. Off to one side a rectangle of light marked the open door of the blacksmith shop. Major Faro and the wounded Lieutenant Miller would be there, he supposed; Lee Howell probably would be with them. Well, that was none of his affair. His job was with the troops.

He had covered perhaps twenty yards when he heard footfalls in the dust behind him and looked over his shoulder to see that a man was following him from the corral. The silhouette of heavy shoulders and the lurching gait told him that it was Clendenning. He was about to go on when the corporal's voice stopped him.

"Henny, that you?" Clendenning called thickly.

Quarterhill didn't answer but there was something in the corporal's voice that made him turn and retrace his steps to the corral. He stopped in front of Clendenning, who stood with his legs spraddled out and the moonlight on his heavy face.

"Aw, Christ," he said disgustedly. "I thought it was Henny—not a goddamn' recruit. Beat it!"

Tiredness lay in Quarterhill like a rock, and he held his temper in check with an effort. He could smell whiskey on Clendenning's breath and that didn't improve his disposition; furthermore, he had a hunch that it had been the corporal, taking the easiest way out, who had turned those troop horses loose in the corral. It was something to make an issue of, anyway.

"Who gave orders to turn those horses into the corral?" he asked, making his voice rough. "Harvey?"

"I done it on my own," Clendenning said, rocking back and forth on the balls of his feet. "You got any objection to it, recruit? Not that I care."

"You're supposed to be an old soldier," Quarterhill retorted, sarcasm in his voice. "Maybe you'd like to explain to a recruit what would happen if the Sioux jumped us tonight."

"You commandin' this troop, Quarterhill?"

"No, I'm not commanding this troop!"

Clendenning spat and Quarterhill could see his slack-mouthed leer in the moonlight. "Then keep your goddamn' smart questions to yourself," he said, and Quarterhill wondered a little at the complacent tone that had crept into his voice now. "Get out of my way—I'm lookin' for Henny!"

Clendenning shouldered his way on by, and Quarterhill stood, looking after him for a moment, a little puzzled by the new cockiness that had come into the man. It could be the liquor, he supposed, but he thought that it was more than that. Clendenning knew something and the knowledge pleased him, he decided. He wondered if it had something to do with Major Mark Faro being in command of Provisional Q Troop now.

He started for the cottonwoods again, the trampled dust of the bench powdery beneath his boots. The moon was well up now, he noted with a gray thoughtfulness; its eerie light made shadowy ramparts of the bastions across the river. He had almost reached the first of the trees when Ed Harvey's voice reached him, coming from the lighted door of the blacksmith shop.

"Quarterhill! That you?"

"It's me," Quarterhill said. "What do you want?"

"I got to have help," Harvey answered heavily, and he came on in the night until he was standing close so that his words no longer carried toward the cooking fires. "The Lootenant Miller is gettin' worse. We got to do something. Come take a look."

"What about your major?"

Harvey spat and a harder note crept into his voice. "All *he* can think to do is to get the lootenant back to McKeogh," he said thinly. "Anyway, I ain't seen him for the last half hour. It's up to you an' me to get that bullet out of Miller, Quarterhill. The lootenant's dead if we don't."

"What's this about Faro getting Miller back to McKeogh, Ed?" Quarterhill asked as they turned back to the blacksmith shop. "The troop's not big enough to provide an escort."

"The whole troop's goin' back, accordin' to Major Faro," Harvey said bleakly. "We ain't marchin' after Hat."

Quarterhill spoke a short, explosive word; then the two of them were silent until they came to the lighted doorway. Harvey led the way in. The smelly lantern still smoked above the forge and the poor light, sifting down across his face, made the officer's features seem sharper and more clearly limned than he had remembered them to be, Quarterhill thought soberly as he knelt on one knee beside the stained pallet.

He lifted the soggy pad which rested on Miller's naked belly. Beneath was a hole, blue and puckered against the lieutenant's startlingly white skin.

"He ain't bled too much," Harvey said, putting a false cheerfulness into his voice which fooled neither of them. "Sometimes that could be a good sign."

"Bleeding inside, probably," Quarterhill grunted. "Give me a hand to turn him, Ed. Easy . . ."

Miller groaned faintly and his eyelids twitched but didn't open as the two of them rolled him on his belly and pulled blue shirt and undershirt away. Quarterhill's fingers, probing as gently as those of a woman now, found the hard lump that the lead slug made beneath the officer's lower ribs. He motioned to Harvey and the two of them rolled Miller onto his back again.

"Well?" Harvey asked, and Quarterhill didn't miss the almost pleading note in the older man's voice. "What do you think? Has he got any chance?"

"The bullet could have curved around his ribs—missed his vital organs," Quarterhill murmured, sitting back on his heels and speaking half to himself. "If we can get the thing out before too much infection sets in, he could have a chance, I think. Not much of one—but still a chance."

"Then we will get that bullet out," Ed Harvey said, and the angry violence that had come into his voice surprised Quarterhill a little. "Because, as long as the Lootenant Miller is alive, I will take my orders from him an' not from any major from Washington. If the lootenant says to march when that time comes, we march, an' we march up the Fourth of July!"

"And if the lieutenant is not alive when that time comes, Ed?" Quarterhill asked softly. "What then?"

"I will know that answer when I have got to know it," Harvey said stolidly. "You've had experience in these things before, I would guess. Gunshot wounds?"

"I've had experience."

"Then you handle the job," Harvey said harshly, getting to his feet. "You are the younger man, Lance Corporal Quarterhill. I will do what you say."

Quarterhill nodded, getting to his own feet. "Send somebody to relieve Garbish. He and Dolliver are at the forks, watching the canyon. We may need him here."

"Right," Harvey grunted and stumped out.

Quarterhill looked across Miller to where the trooper Wheelding leaned against the wall, his face pinched and scared beneath its dirt. He spoke curtly to the man.

"What's your name, soldier?"

"Wheelding, corporal."

"All right, Wheelding," Quarterhill said. "Go rustle me up some hot water. I want a lot of it."

Wheelding sidled around the end of Miller's pallet and went on out into the moonlight. After he had gone, Quarterhill sucked on his dead pipe while he tried to recall all that he had ever known—been told—about gunshot wounds. It would be all too little, he thought regretfully. Then he was aware that Miller's eyes were open now and that the officer was looking at him with a certain understanding in his face.

"Water," he said faintly, slurring the word.

Quarterhill reached for the canteen that Harvey had placed on the anvil block; he knelt again and slid an arm beneath the other's shoulders, lifting him a little so that he could drink. Not good for a man with a belly wound, the back of his mind warned him. The hell with that, he decided. A man with no better chances than Miller had didn't deserve to die thirsty.

"Take it easy, lieutenant," he murmured as he eased the other down again and felt the need to say something to take the loneliness out of the officer's face. "We'll get that bullet out of you soon. Then you'll feel better."

Miller's lips moved again but this time no sound came and Quarterhill could see his eyes grow angry with his efforts to push out the words. He tried again, and finally got his lips around the phrases that came in a halting, husky whisper.

"You're . . . Quarterhill . . ."

"That's right. Take it easy, lieutenant. There's no need to talk."

"Mus' talk." The words were so low that Quarterhill had to bend close to hear. "Give me . . . whiskey . . . mus' talk . . ."

Quarterhill started to say that there was no whiskey—then stopped as he remembered the boozy odor that had been on Clendenning's breath. "I'll be back in a minute," he grunted and came to his feet in a long, easy motion.

He called at the edge of the cottonwoods, and after a moment, Clendenning answered in a surly voice and came to the edge of the shadows. Quarterhill spoke to him in a flinty voice, and there was something in the tone of it that made the big corporal march ahead of him toward the corral.

"Well, what the hell do you want?" he demanded as the two of them halted by the enclosure.

Quarterhill wrapped his fingers in the front of the bigger man's shirt and slammed him hard back against the poles. "I want that bottle you've been nibbling on, Clendenning," he said, his voice rough as a file. "Where is it?"

The corporal's face looked doughy in the moonlight, but he tried to bluster his way out of this. "Gettin' goddamn' big for your britches, ain't you, recruit?" he began, but Quarterhill slapped the rest of the words away with the flat of his hand.

"Either you get that bottle for me or I'll beat your head to a pulp against these poles, God damn you!" he said through his teeth, and the murderous temper behind the words knocked the last of the resistance out of the big corporal. "Where is it?"

"In my saddlebags," Clendenning mumbled.

"Lead me to them," Quarterhill snapped. "Then turn out a detail and get these horses on a picket line! And if you don't think that's an order, you try to argue about it!"

By the heft of it, the bottle was almost half full, Quarterhill thought as he started back for the blacksmith shop. Harvey had returned when he got there; the sergeant stood in the shadows of a corner, moody and withdrawn into himself, and he said nothing as Quarterhill dropped to one knee beside Miller, lifted the officer again, and held the bottle to his lips.

"This rotgut is probably bad enough to squirt that slug the rest of the way through your back, lieutenant," he said in an attempt at grim humor. He hadn't thought that Miller would hear the words, but the officer's eyes opened and there was a wry understanding in them as he managed to get a sip of the neat whiskey down. Quarterhill nodded a hard approval. "Try another, lieutenant. Two won't kill you any quicker than one will."

The wounded man swallowed again—a bigger swallow this time—and a little color was beginning to come back into his gray face as Quarterhill eased him back once more. For a moment Miller lay quietly, letting the liquor work in him. Then he started to speak, his words clearer now.

"Quarterhill," he said huskily. ". . . Odd name . . . remember where I heard it before now . . . letter my mother

110

wrote me from West Point . . . always writing things . . . my mother . . . things about West Point . . ."

Quarterhill sat back on his heels, his face dark and guarded. "Don't try to talk," he said harshly. "You're going to need all of the strength that you've got."

Miller rolled his head from side to side. "Mus' talk," he muttered. "Tell you why in minute . . . Cadet Quarterhill . . . that was it . . . my mother wrote . . . resigned from West Point to go south . . . after Fort Sumter . . . Age would about fit . . . experience . . . everything fits . . . You that Quarterhill?"

Quarterhill considered the question, his face settled into brooding and somber lines. He heard the faint scrape of a step outside; looked up and saw that Lee Howell was framed in the doorway, the lantern light glinting dully on her dark hair. Her eyes were questioning, but she didn't speak, and Quarterhill returned his attention to the man who lay on the pallet.

"I am that Quarterhill," he said harshly.

He didn't miss the satisfaction that showed for a moment in Miller's face. "You served in . . . the Confederate Army?" the officer asked, his voice a little stronger.

"I did."

"What rank . . . what command?"

"I was a captain at Appomattox," Quarterhill answered in a flat voice. "Formerly of Jeb Stuart's command."

"Give me more . . . whiskey," Jacob Miller said in a reedy whisper. That wry humor came again. "Talking . . . is dry work. Mus' talk . . . whiskey helps . . ."

Lee Howell came to kneel beside Quarterhill as he lifted Miller again; her shoulder touched his as Quarterhill held the flask to Miller's mouth once more. He swallowed twice and Quarterhill lowered him again. Quarterhill nodded a silent thanks as Lee got to her feet and went to stand by the anvil block.

Miller was going on now. ". . . don' know what regulations say . . . On own authority I am naming you acting captain . . . you understand, Quarterhill? . . . Own authority . . . but it is enough . . . lawful order . . . You understand? . . ."

111

"I understand," Quarterhill murmured. "Now you had better take it easy, lieutenant."

"Take it easy in a minute . . . not through yet . . . turning command of provisional troop over to you, see . . . You will keep command until relieved by proper authority. . . . Staff officer not proper authority . . . Order, you understand . . ."

Again Quarterhill said, "I understand," but his face was more sober and thoughtful now. He glanced up at Ed Harvey, still standing in the shadow in a corner, and he saw a grim satisfaction reflected in the old man's face.

"Mus' do it this way," Miller said, his voice suddenly angry. "Heard what major said . . . name's Faro . . . He means to go back to Fort McKeogh . . . not troop's mission to go back to Fort McKeogh . . . Mus' go after Hat, you understand?"

Conflicting emotions stirred in Quarterhill as he saw the heroic effort that Jacob Miller was making to hang onto consciousness a little longer. He had hoped never to wear the weight of command again, but now he knew that it could not be shirked. He owed it to himself and he owed it to that ragtag troop bivouacked out beneath the cottonwoods, and he owed it to this man here in the blacksmith shop who was probably dying.

"The troop will march after Hat, lieutenant," he said, the words sounding strange in his own ears. "Try to take it easy now. Everything will be all right."

Miller seemed not to hear as his words continued to come like the rustle of dry leaves in the smoky lantern light. "Troop mus' reach . . . headwaters Fourth of July . . . daybreak day after tomorrow, Captain Quarterhill . . . You mus' get to Hat. . . . He will know you are coming. . . . You will have to fight. . . ."

Trooper Wheelding came with a pail of steaming water and stood in the doorway with his eyes wide and scared as he heard Miller's dry voice going on. "Provisional Troop . . . not a good troop, captain . . . not a good troop . . . All you have to do the job with, though . . . mus' trust you for the rest . . . We are both of West Point, Captain Quarterhill. . . . Should mean something . . ."

Miller's voice trailed off into nothingness; his face slack-

112

ened and a faint peace came into it as his eyes closed. Quarterhill murmured under his breath, "Yes, it should mean something, I suppose," and he was vaguely aware that Lee Howell had come to stand beside him now.

"Is he dead?" she asked soberly.

Quarterhill shook his head as he found the pulse in the other's wrist. "He's still alive. For how long I don't know."

"Are you going to do what he asked, Captain Quarterhill? Pursue Hat up the Fourth of July?"

Quarterhill was a little surprised at the question—more surprised by the title with which she had addressed him. He got slowly to his feet to look down at her.

"I intend to do that, Miss Howell," he said, his voice harder than he had meant it to be. "I have another chore to attend to here first. You had better go. You cannot help, and it will not be a pleasant thing to watch."

He saw Lee's lips flatten out. "I will stay," she said. "At least I can pass bandages."

Outside the blacksmith shop Corporal Clendenning moved cautiously away from the window where he had been watching and listening. His face turned mean as he remembered the feel of Quarterhill's hand against his face back there by the corral earlier. So the bastard thought that he was in command of the provisional troop now, did he? Well, Clem Clendenning meant to see about that, and he wouldn't put all his chips on that sniveling son of a bitch of a major. He had other ways.

Plenty of other ways!

Nobody walked all over a Clendenning, by God! His old pappy back in the West Virginia mountains had taught him that. He'd wait for his chance; then he'd fix that bastard Quarterhill once for all. His pappy had been a good waiter—like that time he'd finally caught Old Man McCabe and his woman up in the hills by the big spring. Pappy had taken care of 'em with two shots from his old squirrel rifle, by God. . . .

Mitch Garbish, who had gotten back to the bench a few minutes before, unhooked the lantern now and placed it on the anvil so that its light seeped down over the unconscious

113

man on the pallet. Trooper Wheelding brought another pail of steaming water and placed it beside the first, where it would be handy to Quarterhill's hands. Quarterhill was on his knees beside Miller, sleeves rolled to his elbows, and he nodded curtly.

"We'll begin," he said.

They rolled the wounded officer gently onto his belly so that the light was yellow against his naked back. Lee Howell knelt, holding his head. Ed Harvey came out of the shadows and the lantern light ran along the keen, slender blade of the knife that he handed to Quarterhill.

"Hold him, Ed."

Quarterhill bent forward, his face set and intent and his hand steady as the blade bit into the flesh. Wheelding choked and dodged out into the night as the first bright blood followed the cut. Trooper Wheelding was young, with fuzz instead of a beard, and he had never seen a man cut before.

It seemed to take an endless time. The blacksmith shop was quiet except for the heavy breathing of the four who worked there. Lee's face was a stark, dead white, but her lips were firm and her eyes were steady as she knelt by the pallet. Cool wind, a hint of rain on its breath, blew through the shop, but sweat beaded Quarterhill's face and dripped from the stubble on his chin. Lee reached to wipe it away. He was unaware as his fingers moved with rough skill, probing with the knife blade.

More minutes went by. Then Quarterhill grunted, "Ah!" with a deep satisfaction. He got the misshapen slug in his fingers and dropped it onto the pallet. "Get me a clean swab and the rest of that whiskey, Mitch."

He cleaned the wound with the whiskey, then packed and bandaged it with strips of white cloth that Lee had torn from her petticoat and placed ready to his hand. They turned the wounded lieutenant, still mercifully unconscious, until he was lying on his back again, finished the bandaging, and Quarterhill finally stood, pushing himself up tiredly.

The whiskey bottle stood beside the lantern, a small dram of the liquor covering its bottom, and Quarterhill scowled at it for a moment. Then he shrugged and reached a big hand for the bottle and lifted it to tip the last of the whiskey

114

down his throat. Then he flung the empty bottle away and breaking glass tinkled in the deep shadows of the blacksmith shop.

"Doctor's orders," he grunted and allowed the corners of his mouth to tip in wry self-derision for a moment, but he could feel some of the tension easing out of him as the liquor warmed his belly. With a faint surprise he realized that the whiskey had a smooth and expensive taste; something quite different from the raw brand of rotgut usually found in a trooper's saddlebags. Well, it didn't matter. He said now to no one in particular, "It's the best that I can do; I hope to God that it is good enough."

11

"We Will Fight Again, Bucko"

Lee Howell was bathing Lieutenant Miller's face, a dull gray beneath its dark stubble of beard now. She paused to ask, "What do you mean to do with him, captain?"

Harvey and Garbish, talking in low voices, filed on out into the moonlight. Quarterhill hitched the lantern back to its wire and leaned against the anvil, his arms folded and a faint scowl on his face as he looked down at the girl.

"He can't stay here," he said. "Neither can you, Miss Howell. I will send the three of you, with a small escort, back to Fort McKeogh. It is the best that I can do."

"Three of us?"

Quarterhill's face hardened a little. "Under the circumstances, I do not think that Major Faro will care to accompany the column up the Fourth of July."

He had been thinking of that, he told himself grimly now. Maybe Mark Faro would accept the graceful out offered him—that of taking the escort back to Fort McKeogh. Maybe he wouldn't. Knowing the man, Quarterhill was inclined to think that he would. He'd take it as the price for Quarterhill's silence about the past, if for no other reason. Quarterhill had given his word to the wounded lieutenant, and he was prepared to pay that price. Well, he'd worry about that when the time came.

"My name is Lee, captain," the girl was saying with no particular expression in her voice. She added, asking the question that Quarterhill had least expected her to ask, "You two have known each other before, I think. Am I right?"

"We have known each other before," Quarterhill said.

"During the war?"

"Yes."

"That seems strange. You were in the Confederate Army. Major Faro was in the Army of the Potomac."

Quarterhill straightened. "Let it go, Miss Howell," he

said, his voice a little rough. "Such things are best left buried. Ask Major Faro, if you wish."

Lee got to her feet and came to stand beside him now. "I will ask Major Faro nothing," she said violently. "In case you didn't already know, Captain Quarterhill, Major Faro is a drunkard and a coward! He fled from the fight at the ranch this morning! He has refused to lead this expedition after Hat! There is nothing too damning about Major Mark Faro that I do not already know—or that I could not guess!"

"I was under the impression that he was a friend of yours, Miss Howell," Quarterhill said, the hard note still in his voice. He added deliberately, "Or something more than a friend."

A slow flush crept up into Lee's face and her eyes were angry. "I knew him in Washington last year," she said, her voice now as hard as Quarterhill's had been. "I found him witty and charming there. Out here I have found him to be something less. Does that answer your question, Captain Quarterhill?"

Quarterhill stayed motionless, looking down at her for a long moment. Then he moved his shoulders slightly, and the tightness had gone out of his voice when he finally answered. "I am sorry, Lee," he said, using her given name for the first time. "Under the circumstances, the trip back to Fort McKeogh may not be pleasant. That cannot be avoided, I am afraid."

The anger had gone out of Lee's voice too as she stood looking up at him, her eyes steady and thoughtful. "You have known war, captain," she said slowly. "You know, with the task that you have ahead of you, that you cannot spare an escort to take us back to Fort McKeogh. Is that not true?"

"It's true," Quarterhill said bluntly. "But even in war you do what you have to do, Lee."

Lee shook her head impatiently. "You don't have to send us back, captain. You can take us with you."

Quarterhill stared at her blankly. "Take you with us— a woman and a wounded man? Are you crazy?"

"No," Lee said tartly. "As for me, forget that I am a woman. I can ride as well as any man. I know the country and I know the plans that my father had for handling Hat.

117

That is more than anyone else in your troop knows, Captain Quarterhill!"

A faint thoughtfulness came into Quarterhill's face. Then he shook his head as he looked soberly at where Jacob Miller lay on his pallet. "He'd never make it, Lee."

"He might have a better chance than he could have trying to get back to Fort McKeogh," Lee said, her voice earnest. "It's two days back to Fort McKeogh. There's a chance that the troops Colonel Bexar wired for will catch up to us sooner than that, captain. They will have a surgeon with them."

Again Quarterhill looked soberly down at her in the smoky light. He was vaguely conscious of the picture that she made. The bramble scratch was dark against the ivory oval of her face; there was a firm and exciting roundness to her beneath the tight-fitting bodice of her gray dress, and there was a pride in the set of her shoulders. He put that thought away from him.

In some ways what she had said made sense, he knew. Provisional Q Troop could not spare any men to send back as an escort to Fort McKeogh. That was the most important thing. On the other hand, he had to think of Lieutenant Miller. . . .

It was the lieutenant who took the decision out of Quarterhill's hands. The wounded officer stirred a little on his pallet, and Quarterhill saw that his eyes were open now. He guessed that the man had been conscious and listening during the past few minutes. Miller's lips moved.

"Miss Howell is right, captain," he said, his voice surprisingly strong. "You will take me with you . . . up the Fourth of July. . . . That is an order, sir. . . ."

Lee knelt to bathe Jacob Miller's face again, and Quarterhill stood for a long moment, looking down at the two of them, his mouth hard and his eyes withdrawn. Miller stared unblinkingly back, and Quarterhill knew that whatever the lieutenant's condition might be a few hours from now, at the moment he was in full possession of his faculties. He had given an order and he meant to have it obeyed, knowing full well the cost to himself.

"Very well," Quarterhill said then in an expressionless tone. "You will accompany the column, sir."

He wheeled abruptly and went out into the moonlight. Ed Harvey was waiting for him by the door, and together they walked a little away from the blacksmith shop.

"I heard what he said," Harvey said in his gritty voice. "It will slow us, but that is better than losing some of the few we have to send an escort back to McKeogh."

"Yes," Quarterhill agreed absently.

"There is a light wagon in the shed," Harvey went on, the tone of his voice a little relieved—as if this was something tangible that he could get his teeth into. "Likely Jensen's harness mules are somewhere about down on the flats. I will send a detail out to look for them."

"Do that. We march at midnight, Ed."

Harvey said, "Right," but trouble had come back into his face now. "Maybe the Lootenant Miller said that you were in command of the provisional troop, an' for me it goes. It will not go so easy with the rest, Quarterhill. They are not goin' to figure that a man can be an acting lance corporal one minute and their commandin' officer the next. . . ."

Harvey's voice trailed off as Quarterhill's mouth flattened out thinly. "I don't expect the troop to like it, Ed," he said, his voice rough. "Also, I don't give a damn whether the troop likes it or not. That's the way that it is for now, and they'll take it that way. You pass that word!"

"I will do that thing," Harvey murmured.

Quarterhill's voice softened. "Don't let things ride you too hard, Ed," he said. "It's my trouble—if it comes."

Ed Harvey nodded soberly as he turned out his salute. "I will make it part of mine, cap'n," he said and wheeled away. The shadows swallowed him.

Quarterhill stood for a moment, watching him go. Then he was aware of a light step behind him and turned. Lee Howell was there, the moonlight touching the oval of her face. She came to stand close beside him, and Quarterhill was aware of the fragrance of her hair as she looked up at him.

"You have burned your bridges behind you, Captain Quarterhill," she said softly. "I think that you are a brave man, for it was a thing that you did not have to do."

"A man is his own best judge of that," Quarterhill answered absently. "I made my own decision."

"What will you do with Mark Faro?"

Quarterhill shrugged. "He can come with us or return to Fort McKeogh as he chooses. I have no interest in what he does, Miss Howell. None whatever."

"It was Lee once this evening," the girl murmured. "Let's leave it that way, captain. Mark Faro will try to make trouble for you, I think."

"He can try," Quarterhill said indifferently.

"He is a vindictive man. He will not forgive you for taking command in his stead. What about when you get back to Fort McKeogh? He has influence in Washington."

"I'm not thinking beyond day after tomorrow," Quarterhill answered roughly. "After Hat has been stopped, it will be time to think further, perhaps."

"Yes," Lee said. "I suppose it will."

She stood there for a moment looking soberly up at him in the moonlight. Then she placed her hands on his cheeks and pulled his head down and kissed him on the mouth, then slipped away from his arms and turned back toward the blacksmith shop.

Over her shoulder she said, "Good luck, Webb Quarterhill. Good luck to all of us."

Troopers Ladue and Jones had picketed their horses in the aspen of a little draw that led up to a knob that rose a hundred feet above the flats. They carried carbines and saddle rolls to the scattered boulders that gave them cover on the knoll's crest. Presently they ate raw bacon and hard bread and washed both down with water, warm and tasting of metal from their canteens. They would not risk a fire here.

It was full dark when they had finished, and Ladue said thinly, "I'll take the first watch. Get some sleep."

He settled himself, back against a rock, where he could look down into the rough country that broke away to the southwest. Amen Jones took his dead pipe from his teeth, stowed it in a pocket, and busied himself with small chores for a moment. Then he moved up the slope to settle onto his heels beside Ladue.

"I'll sit with you for a little, if you ain't got no objection to it," he murmured with a little diffidence in his voice. "I am sorry, Frenchy . . . for this afternoon."

"Let it go," Ladue told him roughly.

Both fell silent, and each knew that the other was thinking of that few minutes when they had stood among the pines above the dry wash earlier while the sunset had painted the sky red in the west. Ladue, a man wanted for killing a gambler in Sunbeam, was remembering the words that Amen Jones had spoken back there on the bench in his mild, unassuming voice.

The French Canadian stirred a little now, the metal of his carbine making a soft clink against the rock. The moon was tipping the sharp shoulders of the mountains, to put vague and uneasy shadows into the cottonwoods below; a little wind, turning cool now and carrying the spicy smell of sage, made a soughing sound in the aspens. There was a peace in the night that was made more poignant by the harsh events of the day.

Ladue broke the silence, his voice a little strange. "Do you believe in the resurrection, Amen?" he asked. "You said something about that . . . back there."

Amen Jones sat for a long moment with his head bent forward a little, and his face was oddly serene in the moonlight. He said slowly at last, "Yes, I believe in it. A man has got to believe in something, I guess, Frenchy."

"I don't believe in nothing," Ladue said harshly. He added in a more gentle tone, "Her name was Susan."

"I know," Amen Jones said.

The silence fell between them again, and both knew that the subject was closed and that neither would open it again. It was better that way. It had to be. For half an hour longer Amen Jones stayed on. The two men spoke only once more in that time, their words a murmur in the shadows.

"What do you think of Quarterhill, Frenchy?" Amen asked. "He's no recruit. He's seen fighting before."

Ladue's answer surprised Amen a little, for the French-Canadian was a slow man to praise anyone. "I'd feel a hell of a lot better about tomorrow's march up the Fourth of July if he was in command of the troop," Ladue said soberly. "I wouldn't give a goddamn what his rank was."

Amen Jones nodded his solemn agreement. He said, "Aye, that goes for me too, Frenchy," and he faded back into the shadows among the boulders. The night settled down.

The moon was an hour's march higher into the sky when Amen was awakened by Ladue's hand on his shoulder. The other man's cautious whisper came in a soft warning as he sat up.

"Something moving in the draw where the horses are," Ladue said. "Cover me while I go for a look."

Amen rolled free of his blanket; picked up carbine and belt, and followed as Ladue led the way to the knob's flank. Here Amen dropped flat behind a boulder, laying out cartridges in a neat row handy to his fingers as Ladue slipped on through the shadows. It was a quarter of an hour later when Ladue's disgusted voice drifted back up the slope.

"Nothin' but a couple of goddamn' mules," he said as he climbed back to the knob. "Harness-broke, by the looks of 'em—probably the ones Jensen used to drive to his spring wagon. I tied 'em with the horses, or we'd be chasin' the four-legged bastards the rest of the night."

Clouds were piled up in dark masses over the canyon of the Fourth of July, and there was the smell of storm in the air, Quarterhill thought absently as he moved across the moonlight toward the corral. The feel of Lee's kiss was still on his lips, but he put that behind him as he forced his mind along familiar but long-unused tracks as the habits of command returned to him.

He checked over what had to be done if Provisional Q Troop was to reach Ghost Basin at the headwaters of the Fourth of July in time. And fight, in all probability, when it finally got there. Provisional Q Troop, undisciplined and untrained. Already time had become a tyrant, and a sense of urgency began to run in him as he counted the few hours that remained to them.

Better than fifty miles to march over rough, backbreaking country; barely thirty hours to do it in, with tired horses and men who could turn mutinous at any moment. A march made harder by the fact that Lieutenant Miller had to be taken along in a wagon across country innocent of any road. Add to that the fact that Hat would doubtless try to ambush the column at some point along the route, and you had a hell of a situation, Quarterhill concluded wryly.

He was surprised that the thought bothered him as little

as it did. Instead, he found that he was buoyed by a quiet elation at the prospect of action ahead. It would be good to be riding at the head of a troop again. Even if it was a ragtag troop that he led and that leadership would not last long.

Furtive movement in the bivouac under the cottonwoods caught his attention now, and he paused, a premonition of trouble sharpening his perceptions. The shadows flowed into shifting patterns over there, and his ears caught the murmur of low voices. Something in their timbre said that here came trouble.

He stopped to watch as half a dozen men separated themselves from the darker background. They spotted Quarterhill in the moonlight now and came toward him. As the distance lessened, Quarterhill recognized the bull-like shoulders and the rocking gait of the ex-pug, Mulroney, in the lead. The smaller man beside him was Tash, the recruit with the sly, weasel-sharp face. The little group halted a few yards away and Quarterhill picked the rest of them out now; they were the worst of the lot that he had ridden with from Jefferson Barracks, he thought as he waited for them to speak. A man called out thickly:

"Go ahead, Tash. Ask the bastard!"

Tash moved forward a little, greasy hair falling down into his eyes as he looked at Quarterhill. There was a certain air of bravado about the skinny man that wouldn't be there if Mulroney wasn't close behind him, Quarterhill guessed.

"Well?" he demanded sharply. "If you've got anything to say, Tash, go ahead and say it!"

"You're goddamn' right I got something to say," Tash answered, his voice rising thinly. "The boys an' me hear that you've set yourself up as a goddamn' officer, now that Miller is down. We hear you're figurin' to march us up the Fourth of July. Us boys would like to know if that's right."

"That's right," Quarterhill said evenly. "Have you got any objections, Tash?"

"You're goddamn' right we got objections!" Tash yelled as he moved closer, Mulroney following and the rest hanging back. "We got a hell of a lot of objections, mister!"

Again Quarterhill caught the smell of whiskey, and he knew, with a quick flash of temper, that the bottle he had taken from Clendenning had not been the only bottle that the corporal had owned. Clendenning wasn't with this crowd, but Quarterhill guessed that he had inspired this incipient mutiny.

He took his time about answering Tash, studying the faces in front of him as he did so. Mulroney was the key to this, he suspected; the ex-pug was to be the instrument that would remove former Captain Webb Quarterhill from any possibility of exercising command. That incident back in the sutler's store at Fort McKeogh was clearer now. His eyes flickered across Mulroney's scarred face briefly. The man stood quietly, he saw, his arms cocked a little and no expression on his battered features.

As if he's waiting for the bell, Quarterhill thought. *This is just another fight to him.*

To Tash, he said, "I'll listen. Make it short."

"He'll listen, he says!" Tash yelled, swinging around to the others. "This high an' mighty Quarterhill that thinks he's a goddamn' officer says he'll listen. Big of him, ain't it!"

"You have thirty seconds left," Quarterhill said.

Tash swung back to him, his face contorted in the moonlight. "Well, *you'll* listen to us, you son of a bitch!" he shouted. "Us boys have taken a vote! We voted that Corporal Clendenning will take command of the troop an' march it back to Fort McKeogh tomorrow, God damn you! Take him, Mulroney!"

Tash jumped aside and Mulroney moved forward, shuffling his big feet in the dust. His hands, doubled into fists, still hung at his sides, but his heavy shoulders were hunched and his chin tucked in. He halted a few feet away and his small eyes watched Quarterhill with no expression in their opaque depths.

"Put up your hands, bucko," he said in his deep, rumbling voice. "I said that we would fight again."

"So you did," Quarterhill murmured.

He had been standing, arms loose at his sides and feet spread a little apart, and now he jumped, covering the distance that separated him from Mulroney in one tigerish leap. He dug a fist deep into the other's heavy belly; as Mulroney doubled over, his breath going out in an explosive grunt, Quarterhill locked his hands and sledged them down against the back of the other's neck, driving the man face down into the dirt.

Mulroney was tougher, faster than Quarterhill had thought. With a surprising agility for so big a man, Mulroney rolled to his feet, spitting dirt, and charged with his big fists flailing. Quarterhill gave ground, sliding away from the blows as he slammed at the roll of fat beneath Mulroney's ear. The ex-pug grunted heavily and came on, boring in.

A blow caught Quarterhill high on the head—exploded a galaxy of stars in front of his eyes as Mulroney's arms reached for him in a clumsy bear's hug. Quarterhill drove a boot heel into the squat man's instep, heard the other's howl of pain as the arms loosened. He smashed again at Mulroney's belly and backed away again, trying to give his head time to clear. The rest of the men, led by Tash, started to surge forward as Tash's voice lifted in a high and snarling sound.

"Get the bastard . . . give him the boot!"

Now Ed Harvey's voice cut sharply through the night behind Quarterhill, the words hard as bullets. "Stand still, the lot of you! Just so much as blink your eyes an' I'll drop you in your tracks, God damn your mangy souls!" The click of a hammer being drawn back gave a wicked punctuation to the words.

If Mulroney heard that, he gave no sign as he rushed again and Quarterhill called sharply, "Take care of the rest of them, Ed. This one's mine!" He slashed at Mulroney's windpipe with the edge of his hand and saw pain and shock roll the man's eyes up beneath his hairless brows for an instant.

It was enough. Quarterhill tipped the other's head around with a hard left hand, sledged his right fist into Mulroney's beefy neck, and smashed a knee into Mulroney's chin as the squat man fell forward. He went on down to his hands and knees and made no effort to get up again as he swung his head back and forth, hoarse and retching noises coming from him in the moonlight.

"Get up, Mulroney," Quarterhill said, his voice savage. "I'd like to hear some more about how you boys voted! Get on your feet and tell me about it, damn you!"

Mulroney made no attempt to obey, and Quarterhill could

125

hear the strained, uneven breathing of the others as they stood there beneath Ed Harvey's gun. He swung around on them, stalking forward stiff-legged while he allowed his black anger to run. They watched him come, sullen uncertainty in place of the bravado that had been in their faces before.

"We'll take another vote right here," Quarterhill said, slapping his words at them wickedly. "Tash, you're a great hand to talk. Let me hear you vote now!"

Tash, his weasel face thoroughly scared behind its curtain of greasy hair, tried to squeeze his way back into the crowd. The others shouldered him out again.

"Well?" Quarterhill demanded.

"It was just a joke," he mumbled.

"And you don't want to vote?"

"No."

"No what, soldier?"

"No, sir."

Quarterhill pointed a finger as if it were a pistol at another man; he was picking the worst of them, those whom Clendenning had palled with. "You, Henny!" he snapped. "Let's hear from you. Maybe you'd like to vote again!"

Henny managed a loose grin in the moonlight. "Hell, cap'n," he said, "I just come along for the ride an' the free liquor. Be a captain if you want to—it's all right with me."

Quarterhill stood in front of them a moment longer, his battered knuckles on his hips as he watched each man's eyes drop beneath the dark rage of his stare. This had come sooner than he had expected, but that was just as well, he was thinking coldly. He might just as well have a full showdown now; either he took command now or he didn't take command at all.

"Sergeant Harvey," he said, the parade-ground rasp rough in his voice, "march these men back to the bivouac area. Fall the troop in there and call the roll. I want every man present except those on outpost. I'll be there presently."

Ed Harvey wheeled in front of Quarterhill; he saluted stiffly and said, "Yes, sir," in a voice that was thin with satisfaction. Wheeled back to bark harshly, "All right, you kitchen scum! Form up! Two of you give a hand to Mister Mulroney. . . . He ain't feelin' well, it seems!"

12

Into Fourth of July Canyon

Quarterhill watched as they filed off in the moonlight, then turned toward the corral. Clendenning hadn't stretched a picket line as he'd been told, he noted. Just another minor crime to be added to the long list that Clendenning had to answer for, Quarterhill thought dispassionately. He meant to take Clendenning's stripes away from him in front of the troop. Legally, he hadn't a leg to stand on. Once they were back at Fort McKeogh, Clendenning's rank would doubtless be restored; former Lance Corporal Webb Quarterhill would, in all probability, be in the guardhouse.

But the hell with that! Until they *were* back at Fort McKeogh, Webb Quarterhill's word was going to be law in Q Troop, and Q Troop was about to find that out, by God.

It was ten minutes later when Quarterhill finished his rounds of the corral and roughed out in his mind plans for the march up the Fourth of July. The troop was drawn up in a double line, standing at a stiff attention as Quarterhill returned to the cottonwood grove. The embers of a fire glowed redly at one side, and he kicked loose brush over the coals so that flames flared up to send a flickering light over him as he took his post. Ed Harvey faced about, lifting his hand in a stiff salute.

"Provisional Troop present or accounted for except for Corporal Clendenning, sir," he said.

Quarterhill returned the salute with an easy gesture, the back of his mind thinking: *How easy it is to fall into the old habits without even trying.* Aloud, he asked in clipped tones, "Where is Corporal Clendenning, sergeant?"

"I ain't been able to find him nowhere in the camp, sir," Ed Harvey answered heavily. "If the cap'n wants, I'll take a detail and search the bench."

"Let it go for now," Quarterhill said curtly. He moved forward a little so that the firelight fell across the rock-hard lines of his face as his eyes ranged deliberately along the double line of men. He said then, his words as rough as broken glass, "I am Captain Webb Quarterhill, formerly of Jeb Stuart's command. Under proper authority, I have assumed command of this troop. At midnight we march up the Fourth of July after Hat. Obey orders and behave like soldiers, and I will get along. Step out of line by so much as an inch and I'll crucify you, by God!"

He stopped and took his time about letting his hard stare range along the line of faces once more. The men stood at their frozen attention as he deliberately allowed the silence to lengthen. At the far left he saw the firelight glinting across Mulroney's battered face and hairless brows. The squat man was staring back at him with an expressionless stolidity.

Quarterhill said abruptly then, "First sergeant!" and was about to tell Harvey to dismiss the troop when he heard the sound of unsteady footsteps coming up behind him and saw a subtle change come over the faces in front of him. He turned, not hurrying his movement, and saw that Mark Faro—a smirking Clendenning at his elbow—had halted in the moonlight behind him.

Faro stood there, swaying a little on his feet and his mouth a little triumphant with the courage that the liquor had put into him. Quarterhill waited; he'd let the other start this, he decided. Faro took a step forward, and now he aimed a forefinger at Quarterhill as his voice rose, his words slurring a little. His eyes didn't meet Quarterhill's own.

"Your name's Quarterhill," he shouted. "You're a God-damned Rebel. Don't try to deny it!"

"And you're the man who broke his parole, major," Quarterhill answered softly. "Maybe you'd like to tell these men about that. They're plain soldiers, but they'd understand."

He saw that his words had gotten through the drunken haze that held Faro; the man still had a little shame left in him, Quarterhill thought. He seemed to grow smaller as he stood there. He dropped his arm uncertainly. Clendenning moved forward now so that the light fell across his heavy,

128

dly assured face. This thing was not going the way he had planned it.

"Major," he said, pitching his voice so that it carried to the men still standing at attention, "you ain't goin' to take no lip from a goddamn' recruit, are you? Is he a recruit or ain't he, boys?" He turned a little to throw the question at the others . . . then Quarterhill was beside him—spun him around.

With a quick hand, he ripped the badly sewn chevrons from Clendenning's sleeves and tossed them into the last of the dying fire. "Sergeant Harvey!" he said through his teeth.

"Yes, sir!" Harvey said, moving forward.

"This man is a private and in arrest from now on," Quarterhill said. "He will lead you to where he has his liquor hidden, and you will bring it here at once. If he gives you any argument, shoot him! Do you understand?"

Hard satisfaction showed briefly in Harvey's craggy face. He dropped a hand to the butt of the gun at his hip and said, "Yes, sir. I understand. Come on, you!"

The two disappeared into the shadows, and Quarterhill turned his back deliberately on Faro as he faced the troop again. The watching men were still frozen at attention, their faces a little awed by what they had seen and by the deadliness in Quarterhill's voice. He let the silence grow again."

Then he said, "Private Garbish!"

Garbish answered, "Yes, sir," and stepped forward, a deep thoughtfulness replacing the usual good humor in his face.

"As of now, you are acting corporal in Clendenning's place," Quarterhill said curtly. "That's all."

"Yes, sir," Garbish said again and stepped back.

Clendenning, his face ugly with fear and anger, came back into the last of the firelight, carrying the cowhide bag, with Ed Harvey goading him grimly on from behind. The two halted as Quarterhill whirled on them.

"That's all of the stuff, cap'n," Harvey said.

"Good," Quarterhill answered harshly. To Clendenning, he said, "Open it and smash the bottles against that rock!"

A sound like an animal in pain came from the shadows where Faro stood as Clendenning wrenched the bag open and lifted out a bottle. "No!" Faro said in a strangled voice.

"Oh, my God . . . no!" He started to lurch forward, but Quarterhill caught him with a big hand and flung him roughly back. Faro went to his hands and knees and crawled back into the shadows as the first bottle smashed.

Light glinted faintly on the heap of broken glass and the night was heavy with the smell of whiskey as Clendenning finished his unwelcome task. He flung the cowhide bag away from him and faced Quarterhill with his shoulders heaving.

"You're goin' to pay for that, by God!" he said hoarsely. "You're goin' to pay good for that, you son of a bitch!"

Quarterhill struck him across the face, rocking the bigger and heavier man back onto his heels. "Listen to me, Clendenning," he said, his voice wicked. "I'm not going to tell you again. You get in my way just once more and I'll stand you in front of a firing squad and have you shot!"

A stir, like a little shiver, ran through the ranks of Provisional Q Troop. Then Mulroney's heavy voice, a malicious satisfaction in it, broke the silence.

"An' Mulroney's the lad who'll volunteer to pull a trigger on that firin' squad, bucko—I mean cap'n."

Quarterhill heard the faint ripple of laughter that stirred the ranks in front of him, and he relaxed as he felt the tension begin to ease. The troop was his from now on, he knew. Ed Harvey came at his nod.

"Dismiss the troop, sergeant," he said. "We'll march in an hour. What about those mules?"

"Bliss an' Dougherty found 'em at Ladue's outpost," Harvey answered, and he swung about to call, "Dismissed!"

Mark Faro came out of the shadows as the men scattered. His voice was steadier now; the events of the past few minutes had sobered him some, Quarterhill guessed.

"You're not going to get away with this, Quarterhill," Faro said, his words cold and angry. "Once we get back to Fort McKeogh I'm going to have you tried for every crime in the book! Don't think that I won't!"

"Even with your own record, major?" Quarterhill asked softly. "Well, it will be your privilege."

"Don't think that you can hide behind something that happened during the war," Faro said violently. "It'll be your word against mine—the word of a Rebel. . . ."

His words trailed away as the assurance went out of his voice. Mark Faro had suddenly remembered those precious bottles that had been wantonly smashed against a rock. With bleak certainty he knew of the horror that lay ahead of him in the next few days. His voice choked and he turned away.

"I will worry about that when the time comes, Major Faro," he heard Quarterhill saying behind him. "That is not now—we may never get back to Fort McKeogh."

Quarterhill, Mitch Garbish and Ed Harvey with him, issued his final orders for the march as the three stood by the corral, where the troop was saddling up. In addition to Garbish, Quarterhill had named Ladue and Dolliver acting corporals; Amen Jones would drive the wagon carrying Lee Howell and the wounded Jacob Miller. Ladue, with a new point, would scout out in front of the column. Flankers would move out as needed.

"We've got a hell of a long way to go," Quarterhill said curtly. "Around fifty miles, and the going will be all bad. There will be nothing but short halts from now on."

"A long march an' a long war," Garbish murmured, unbothered by the prospect. "All of my wars have been long; it's the way that I like 'em, Reb."

Ed Harvey gave Garbish a swift, irritated glance in the moonlight. He started to say that such was no way for an acting corporal to address his commanding officer, then thought better of it. Quarterhill showed no resentment, and Mitch wouldn't use the term except when they were alone, Harvey knew. He'd best let well enough alone.

"This won't be one of your long wars, Mitch," Quarterhill was saying absently. "If we don't get to the Basin before daybreak day after tomorrow, the war's liable to be all over for us in a hurry. Once Hat ties in with the Teton Sioux, a bigger outfit than Q Troop wouldn't stand a chance."

He paused a moment to let his glance slide across the shifting pattern in the moonlight before him . . . troopers leading saddled horses out, men thrusting carbines into saddle boots . . . a pattern he had seen often before on other nights and in other and more distant places . . .

Garbish murmured, "I wouldn't bet on Q bein' in the Basin on time, Reb. Q ain't much."

Quarterhill's mouth flattened out. "If there's a horse that can stand or a man that can ride, he will be in the Basin before the sun comes up the day after tomorrow. You can both pass that word along!"

Ten minutes later Ed Harvey sang out his command, "Prepare to mount . . . Mount!" and Quarterhill, sitting his own horse, heard the familiar creak of saddle leather and the grunting complaint of horses as troopers settled heavily into their saddles. At one side Amen Jones, high on the wagon seat, spoke to his mules as he waited to turn to swing them into their place in the column. Harvey swung about and made his report.

"Troop formed, sir."

"Take your post, sergeant," Quarterhill said, the old rasp of command coming easily into his voice. "Column of twos . . . walk . . . hooooo . . ."

The line flowed into column, splitting to let the wagon in, and the leading files dipped down the slope of the bench that led to the moonlit river. On the far side the canyon of the Fourth of July opened a narrowing V to the north, its broken rims climbing steeply toward the far bastions of the Galenas. Clouds were banking heavily in the northwest and the smell of a coming storm was stronger in the night wind.

For a moment Quarterhill sat watching the column slip into its ordered pattern. It was for this that he had come back into the Army; now he knew that his decision had been right and good. This was the thing that he had always known: the clatter of shoe iron against rocks, the creak of saddle leather and the clank of fighting gear. The low murmur of troopers' voices drifting back as they cursed the march without rancor or made profane comments on the night with the well-what-the-hell-did-you-expect-anyway resignation that is as old as soldiering.

Trumpeter Riviera, his horn slung, pushed his horse up on Quarterhill's left, and the two of them moved out at a trot to pass Mitch Garbish, riding right guide at the head of the first squad. Presently they came to the water, where Ladue waited with his five men. Quarterhill motioned them on with a swing of his arm, and heard the snort of the horses as they struck the water, splashing it up in drops turned to silver by the moonlight.

Provisional Q Troop was on its way.

It was around four in the morning when the storm broke. For the last two hours the troop had been climbing higher into the Galenas across a series of rocky meadows, but the valley was narrowing and patches of rock slide slowed the pace. Quarterhill was riding beside Mitch Garbish at the head of the column as the first fork of lightning split the sky and the crash of thunder banged back and forth between the walls ahead.

"A night march in the rain," Garbish said, his words whipped by a gust of wind as the first rain came down. "It is the way that my luck runs, friend Quarterhill."

Quarterhill didn't miss the new, strange note that had come into Garbish's voice. In the short time that he had known this man, he now thought, he had found Garbish a cheerful adventurer, unbothered by a past tinged with a rogue's paintbrush—uncaring of anything that might lie ahead. He might not have noticed the resignation that ran through Garbish's words now, had not his own dark premonitions of the afternoon returned tonight to ride his shoulders with a heavy weight.

He tried to shake them off.

Fresh thunder threw its cannonade down the canyon. In the flickering flashes of the lightning, the Fourth of July showed its white water as it rushed against the rocky wall to the left. Quarterhill's mount danced nervously, caroming against Garbish's horse as the sky opened up and the rain came down in sheets. Quarterhill steadied the horse with knee and rein.

"Not spooked by a little storm, are you, Mitch?" he asked, raising his voice against the rush of the wind. "Since when have night marches made your luck run worse?"

Garbish refused the invitation of the words; the high good humor that usually ran in him was absent now as he answered. "A hell of a life, Reb," he said heavily. "On a night like this a man should be snug in bed with his woman beside him. He is a fool to be sky-hootin' about the hills with nothin' but grief waitin' for him at the end of the trail."

"Forget it," Quarterhill grunted a little impatiently. "Nobody put a bayonet into the middle of your back and made you hold up your hand when you took the oath again. With the sun tomorrow your luck will be back."

"Fine words, friend Quarterhill," Garbish retorted. "You should have been a preacher . . . but don't give that guff to me. A man knows when his luck's run out. Mine has."

The way climbed to a bench running along the eastern wall fifty feet above the brawling creek. Sparse pine and fir grew here, and if Lieutenant Miller's hand-drawn map was right, this was the last of the good going, Quarterhill knew. Ahead, the Fourth of July rushed through a series of gorges separated by rock slides and eroded gullies that fell from the rims above. They had come a dozen miles since midnight, Quarterhill estimated; there were better than thirty miles of marching still ahead—marching that would be snail-slow until they reached the basin where this tumultuous stream had its beginnings. And time was running out fast.

Too fast.

The rain came down steadily as the column, mud-spattered and weary, came to the north end of the bench. A thicker stand of pine offered a little shelter here, and Quarterhill ordered a halt and passed the word to picket and loosen saddle girths. The troop would rest here an hour. Ladue's party was a quarter of a mile ahead, Riviera riding as connecting file, and Quarterhill sent word up for the point to outpost the halt, then waited for Ed Harvey to come up from the rear of the column.

"Let the men light fires, Ed," Quarterhill said curtly. "This will be the last long halt and the last chance they'll have to get hot grub into their bellies. I'm going up to see Ladue; you'll be in charge here until I get back."

"Right," Harvey said, and Quarterhill caught the tiredness in his voice. "How far you guess we come, cap'n?"

Damn it, Quarterhill thought with a quick irritation, *Harvey's a soldier—he can guess, as well as I can, the number of miles we have covered.* Then he checked the sharp retort that was on his lips as he realized that what Ed Harvey wanted was a little of that assurance from his officer that he'd been accustomed to through all the years of his service. It was little enough for a man to ask, he supposed.

"Maybe fifteen miles, Ed," he said. He added wryly, "Don't let it bother you; we've got plenty of miles left ahead of us. We'll not run out of them any time soon, boy."

He saw Harvey muster a sour grin as he swung up into the saddle again in the rain and turned his horse's head up the canyon. If Hat was planning an ambush, he'd spring it sometime during the coming day, Quarterhill thought as he rode. That was his reason for going to see Ladue. It was going to be up to the French Canadian and his five men to see that Provisional Q Troop was not caught with his head stuck squarely into a noose. . . .

13

Gunfire in the Afternoon

Amen Jones had pulled the light wagon under a pine that was bigger than the rest, where there was a little shelter from the slanting drive of the rain. He unhitched here and led his mules down to water. Lee Howell climbed stiffly down from the wagon bed and stood for a moment looking off into the gray, cheerless dawn while she tried not to hear the snatches of disconnected sentences that spilled from Jacob Miller's lips. For the last hour the fever had been creeping more deeply into him.

Sometimes he was back at West Point; he would talk in his delirium to Quarterhill, recalling things that both of them had once known. Then West Point would slip away and Jacob Miller would be back on the frontier, fighting innumerable unimportant little skirmishes while the big war—the opportunities for promotion and command—were passing him by. Occasionally he talked with a girl named Margaret at Fort Laramie, and occasionally he spoke with Colonel Felix Bexar back at Fort McKeogh. But mostly he spoke with former cadet Quarterhill.

As Lee watched now, Miller pushed himself up a little on an elbow to say, his words suddenly clear, "You cannot treat with Hat, Captain Quarterhill. You must hit him hard. . . ."

Lee moved until she could put a hand on the wounded man's hot forehead and push him gently back down again. *It was a mistake to bring him on this march,* she thought soberly. *A mistake that I helped to make. We should have gone back to Fort McKeogh. How can he ever live through another twenty-four hours of this? And suppose that there is no doctor with the relieving column?*

Questions, but no answers.

Miller lay back, a chill shaking him now, and Lee tucked the blankets more tightly about him. Amen Jones had taken off the officer's boots, jacket, and trousers before they'd left Jensen's, in an effort to make the lieutenant as comfortable as they could. The blankets were soaked with rain now, and they did little to ease the icy spasms that racked the wounded man.

Lee said, angry at the emptiness of her words, "Just rest, lieutenant. Captain Quarterhill knows his business. He will take good care of Hat in time."

"Yes," Jacob Miller said, his eyes opening to stare up into the drip. "I remember now . . . You're Cadet Quarterhill . . . class of sixty-two . . . odd name . . . My mother wrote me . . . You must take care of the troop . . . Cadet Quarterhill . . . It needs a strong man . . . not a very good troop, you see. . . ."

A twig snapped behind Lee and she turned, hoping that it was Webb Quarterhill who was coming. Instead, Mark Faro stood a few feet away in the coming dawn. His expensively cut uniform was sodden and smeared with mud, but despite that, there was a dapper assurance about him. It was a role that Faro had forced himself to assume because he knew that his only chance was to convince Lee Howell to fall in with his plans. If he failed, he knew with a dark certainty that this was the end of the road for Mark Faro. And there was barely enough time left; he must not waste it.

The bottle that he had gotten from Clendenning last night was almost half empty now. He'd been hoarding it with miserly care, taking a tiny sip only when he could no longer deny the screaming demands of nerves that seemed to prickle all over his body. With a vast effort he controlled the shudders that ran through him now and then. He tried not to think of those precious bottles that Quarterhill had caused to be smashed back there among the cottonwoods on the bench.

He couldn't afford to think of that now. He must concentrate, instead, on the plan that he had, if the dark pit was not to engulf Mark Faro forever. Somehow he must manage to get back to the stage station at Doxy before the last of his time had run out; better still, perhaps he might find a bottle that had been overlooked in the ruins at Jensen's. But he needed a guide—Lee Howell. The wounded Miller would be his excuse.

"Lee," he said.

Lee stood still, one hand on the wagon bed as she watched him come closer. "What do you want?" she asked in a tone that showed no feeling for Faro one way or another.

Faro stopped close beside her. "This is all wrong, Lee," he said, and she could smell the stale odor of liquor on his breath now. "It's utter madness for you to be here accompanying the column like this. Worse, it's suicide for Lieutenant Miller! You can surely see that!"

Lee started a sharp retort, then repressed it as Jacob Miller groaned again from his hard bed in the wagon. The uncertainty that she had felt earlier came back to her now.

"What else is there to do?" she asked.

Faro's face darkened as he reached out to put a hand on her arm. "Quarterhill should never have permitted you to start in the first place," he said, rushing his words so that they slurred a little. "He will answer to me for that when we get back to Fort McKeogh. Now I must take you and Miller back."

"It was my suggestion that we accompany the column," Lee said, but much of the conviction had gone out of her voice. "It was Lieutenant Miller's order that we do so, Mark."

"The man was out of his head," Faro said violently. "I know what is best. We'll turn back; it's not too late. I'll order that soldier to harness the mules. We can be back at Jensen's by ten o'clock and on the road to Doxy."

Lee bit her lip in indecision as she stared through the rain into the gray dawn. Faro's words were convincing; was he right and had she and Webb Quarterhill been wrong? she wondered. Did she dare make a second mistake if she *had* been wrong? Then she remembered the selfishness that she had seen in this man in front of her from the start, and she knew, with a sudden clarity, that he was not acting from any consideration for the wounded Lieutenant Miller. He was acting for himself, and that smell of whiskey on his breath gave her a hint as to what his reason was.

"No," she said steadily. "It is too late to go back now. We will go on with the column."

She saw the faint madness that came into Faro's eyes and would have stepped back, had not the wagon prevented her from doing so. Faro had both hands on her arms now and was pulling her toward him. He was suddenly terribly strong.

"You've got to do it, Lee!" he was saying, his words running into one another. "If not for Miller, you've got to do it for me! For *me*, you understand!"

"I'll do nothing for you, Mark. . . ."

The words died in her throat as he pulled her roughly against him now and bent her back against the wagon as his lips sought her mouth. She tried to beat at his face with her fists but he caught her arms and smothered them in his close embrace. She thought frantically: *He's gone mad . . . completely mad . . .*

Then Webb Quarterhill's hard voice was welcome in her ears. "Let her go, Faro," it said.

Faro released her with a suddenness that left her sagging against the wagon, her knees weak. She caught a glimpse of the man's face as he whirled, and saw that it was crazy now. Faro's hand dropped to the holster at his belt; it came up with a gun that unsteadily covered Quarterhill. Faro's voice was thin and wicked as he flung out his words.

"I'd enjoy killing you, Quarterhill. Just give me the hint of an excuse and I'll do that! Miss Howell and I are taking the wagon back to Jensen's. Don't get in our way!"

Quarterhill hit him—a blow that smashed beneath Faro's heart—and he sagged to his knees, then crumpled into a heap without a sound. Quarterhill gave him no further attention as he moved up to the wagon. His eyes were on Miller.

"How is he?" he asked, his voice wholly impersonal.

Lee thought angrily: *He believes that I fell in with Mark's scheme—that I was deliberately letting him make love to me! Well, let him think that if he wishes!*

She said aloud, her voice cold, "He's delirious—out of his head most of the time. He asks for you."

"Why?" Quarterhill asked, scowling. "I can do no more for him, Miss Howell. His nursing is up to you."

"I am quite able to understand that," Lee said curtly.

139

"You ride people roughly, Captain Quarterhill. Is that something that you take pleasure in?"

Quarterhill stood looking down at her for a moment, his face settled into a repose that was a little sad. Again he was acutely aware of the full desirability of this woman; he knew, with a bleak sureness, that she was not for him. A moment ago he had struck an officer. Once the matter of Hat had been settled, Webb Quarterhill had only two choices open to him. He could desert and spend the rest of his life running from the Army—or he could return to Fort McKeogh and an Army jail. Well, the choice was one that didn't have to be taken now. It was a choice that he would make when the time came.

"I have taken pleasure in little since I left Fort McKeogh, Miss Howell," he said in a flat voice, then wheeled and went on to disappear into the gray curtain of mist.

By midmorning the canyon had narrowed to a tight V, so that it was necessary to follow the creek bed as it climbed. A dozen times before noon, Dolliver's squad had to haul the wagon with drag ropes to help the mules. It still rained —a steady, seeping drip out of a sky the color of lead. It turned clay slopes into treacherous chutes and laid slick traps among the rock slides where men and horses floundered and too often fell.

By noon two men were afoot, their horses shot after falls had left them with broken legs. The sound of the shots had been muffled by the high, narrow walls, but they could still carry to any hostile ears that might be listening, Quarterhill knew grimly. It was a chance that he had to take. You didn't leave your animals down and helpless even in enemy country.

At one o'clock the rain stopped and Quarterhill halted the column to eat raw bacon and soggy bread washed down with icy water from the creek. The stream was only a fraction of its former size now, but a long twenty miles still lay ahead to Ghost Basin, Quarterhill guessed soberly as he moved to investigate the dark gorge opening a hundred yards in front. Twenty miles of country like this was a hell of a long way to go, with the juice running out of men and horses and night coming at them too fast.

He put his horse into the stream bed, splashing around boulders as big as cabins that had fallen from the rims above; he picked his way for a quarter of a mile along a shelf that clung to the left-hand wall. Then he saw the cliffs open up again where a big slide had spilled in here as the valley began to widen once more. Ladue and his men waited here where the creek made a sharp bend so that they had a view of the country for a mile ahead. Benches rose in ragged steps toward the rims and spruce and fir studded the steep slopes.

Quarterhill nodded a greeting and stepped down from his horse. He got bacon and a little coffee from his saddlebags and sat on a heel, chewing the two of them together as he spoke to Ladue. The lean French Canadian squinted as he wiped the water from the stubble on his face.

"That's one that I ain't seen before," he murmured as Quarterhill stuffed more bacon and coffee into his mouth. "You learn that in the Reb Army, captain?"

Quarterhill gave him a look that held faint amusement. "We saw damned little coffee in the Rebel Army, Frenchy," he grunted. "Chicory was a luxury; most of the time it was roasted acorns. I don't like the looks of that bench country ahead. Hat could hide fifty braves on either side."

"I've felt eyes peeking down on me for the last ten miles," Ladue said without emotion. "They could jump us any time. Hat's no fool. If he thinks he can hurt us, he'll do it."

"He can hurt us, all right," Quarterhill said quietly. "Don't let yourself get surprised, Ladue. I'll send Carbish up with his squad if you run into trouble."

Ladue gave Quarterhill a bright, hard glance, then returned his attention to the benches ahead. "Whatever you say," he agreed dispassionately. "How soon do we move out?"

"Another ten minutes," Quarterhill told him, and moved back to his horse. "Send a man back if you spot anything."

It was midafternoon and the benches were behind them now, and Quarterhill, easing tired legs in the stirrups, felt a small wave of relief begin to run in him. Ahead, the country was broken by high-backed ridges, the sides patched with timber as they climbed toward the main shoulders of the Galenas—hard country and slow to cross, but it offered less chance for ambush and surprise than had the narrower valley. It would be dark in another three hours, Quarterhill was thinking as he led the column across a meadow fanning from the mouth of a feeder gulch.

The single shot, putting its wicked crack into the gray afternoon, jerked him out of his thoughts. It was followed by five more, their hollow echoes clapping against his eardrums. Then he saw Riviera, pushing his tired horse hard, come out of the willows half a mile upstream. Quarterhill threw up an arm to halt the column and rode on to meet the trumpeter.

Riviera hauled up his blowing horse as Quarterhill neared him. "Injuns," the trooper said, showing Quarterhill a flash of white teeth against the olive tan of his face. "Plenty of 'em. Ladue says to come a-runnin', cap'n."

"I'll have a look," Quarterhill grunted. "Ride back and tell Harvey to hold the troop where it is but to send Garbish and his squad up . . . and leave a little bottom in that horse, son. He's got to take you over a hell of a lot of country yet."

Riviera's even teeth flashed whitely again. "Yes, sir," he said. "I'll be back up with you in a minute."

He was gone again, back to where the column waited. Quarterhill put his own horse into a trot, coming presently to the willows. The sound of Ladue's carbines made spasmodic echoes in the afternoon; they were answered by shots and shrill whoops coming from a low ridge that thrust a long finger into the valley ahead. The willows thickened and a trooper named Ludlow, left as a horse holder, called excitedly across to Quarterhill.

"Over here, cap'n!" The words tumbled over one another. "Frenchy an' the rest are up ahead!"

Quarterhill dismounted, lifting the carbine out of the boot as he tossed his reins to Ludlow. A hundred yards ahead, deployed where a rocky outcrop afforded a little cover, he found Ladue and the other four firing carefully at the ridge. He crouched beside the acting corporal.

"How many?" he asked tersely.

"Twenty-five or thirty, far's I can figure," Ladue grunted.

"Scattered in the brush on that ridge. Hard to get a clean shot at the bastards."

Quarterhill assessed the ground with the quick skill of long practice and made his plan swiftly. "Keep on pecking away at them from here," he told Ladue. "Use up no more ammunition that you have to, but keep them busy. I'll take Garbish and his squad on foot up the gully to the top of the ridge. When you hear our fire, come on up. Got it?"

"We're your boys," Ladue said laconically.

Time—and we've got so damned little of it, Quarterhill's mind reminded him bitterly half an hour later as he led Mitch Garbish and eight men into the last climb on their long swing onto the ridge. *Time is more valuable than bullets right now. I should have been Joshua to command the sun to stand still.*

They came onto the ridge finally, breathing hard, and Quarterhill rested them for five minutes while he crawled forward to where he could see the curve of the ridge below him. Now and then he caught sight of breechclouted, copper-skinned shapes that sifted ghostlike through the brush. The yelling was growing louder as Ladue and his party returned a slow and deliberate fire. The Sioux were working their courage up for a rush, Quarterhill guessed. It was time to go.

"Follow me," he called back softly. "Keep spread out and shoot only when you've got something to shoot at."

It was surprisingly easy. This was a war party of young, untried bucks, and the sudden, accurate fire opening in their rear was a thing that they hadn't expected and didn't know how to meet. Quarterhill's squad moved in; Ladue and his men, reinforced by Dolliver's squad, which Ed Harvey had sent forward, squeezed a tight pincers on the war party, already caught off balance. Half a dozen Sioux went down; the rest faded back up the canyon, and after a little, the hammer of running ponies died slowly away as the gray afternoon began to slip into early evening.

The squads were reassembling by the creek as Quarterhill moved toward where he had left his horse. The quick undercurrent of excitement in the voices of the men told him what he wanted to know. Raggle-taggle Q Troop had its tail up now. This little fight on the ridge had wiped away the shame of yesterday—that debacle at the crossing of the Sleepy Wind. In the past two hours these men had become soldiers. They knew it and they took proper pride that it should be so.

But the troop had paid a price for its blooding.

A trooper named Bliss was dead; two others had flesh wounds, painful but not crippling. Mitch Garbish had taken a Sioux arrow through the calf of his leg. Quarterhill came to where Garbish sat in the brush, swearing with a solid violence as Riviera broke off the feathered end and drew the rest of the shaft on through. Quarterhill dropped down on one knee beside the trooper and knotted a bandage with hard, sure fingers.

"Not too bad," he said to Garbish, "but you'll ride in the wagon from here on in."

"I'll be goddamned if I will," Garbish answered, pain making his voice rough. "Maybe my luck's run out, but it still ain't bad enough to set me to ridin' in no wagon on my ass like some big, fat colonel's wife, by God!"

Quarterhill started to answer, stopped as two of Ladue's men came through the brush, awkwardly carrying the unconscious sergeant between them. The French Canadian had been shot through the chest and the bloody froth on his lips told Quarterhill that the bullet had pierced a lung—that Ladue was likely done for. He felt a hot anger run through him.

"Put him hown here to wait for the wagon," he said, his voice harsher than he meant it to be as he got to his feet. "I guess you're right, Mitch. The wagon won't hold three. Dolliver will have to take over Ladue's point."

Garbish hunched himself around, his bandaged leg thrust straight out in front of him as he looked at the unconscious Ladue. A heaviness had settled into Mitch's face, washing away all of the good humor that had once been there.

"Him an' me have drunk a lot of beers together," he said, half to himself. He allowed his breath to go out gustily as he looked back at Quarterhill now. "I'll take over Frenchy's job, friend Quarterhill. It is a little debt that I figure that I owe him. The payment will be small enough."

For a long moment Quarterhill soberly returned Garbish's rough stare. *It is always the best ones that go first,* he was

144

thinking with a sort of a resigned sadness. *It has to be so—it can be no other way. They are the ones who put themselves where the going is the hardest and the danger the greatest.*

"Can you do it with that leg, Mitch?"

"I can do it."

"Move out as soon as you can. We'll march as soon as I get back to the column. Good luck, Mitch."

14

Daybreak in Ghost Basin

Night came down, a slow fading of the gray daylight into darkness. There'd be no moon tonight; clouds still hung their heavy masses above the canyon, threatening more rain. Q Troop marched dismounted, leading jaded horses as the column stumbled on at a snail's pace. Quarterhill turned his own mount over to Riviera and ranged back along the marching files, legs aching from his own weariness as he urged the others on.

The hourly ten-minute halts became twenty-minute halts—lengthened to half an hour. By midnight the column was marching ten minutes and resting ten. It was the best he could do, Quarterhill thought dully as he stumbled back through the pitch-darkness to where Ed Harvey was trying to keep the march closed up. He found the old man propped against a pine, and there was a hint of defeat in Harvey's voice as he spoke.

"By God, I'm so damn' tired I don't dare set down, cap'n," he said. "If I did, I'd never get on my feet again. This outfit ain't got much marchin' left in it."

"It'll not have to march much longer," Quarterhill told him, and both knew that was a lie; it was a hell of a long way to the Basin yet. How far, neither had any idea. All they could do was keep on going and hope. "We'll make it, Ed."

Harvey's voice lifted querulously in the dark. "An' what if we do? This drag-ass troop won't have nothin' left to fight with even if we do get there. We're through. Down the drain."

"Want to ride in the wagon, Ed?" Quarterhill asked softly. "I know that you're an old man. . . ."

He heard Harvey's outraged grunt, and managed a thin

chuckle as he pictured the offended distaste in the other's face. His suggestion had the effect that he had wanted, because Harvey's voice had its familiar grittiness when he answered.

"You know what you can do with your goddamn' wagon! And I ain't so old that I won't be ridin' where I belong when we find Hat. . . . No wet-nose lance corporal, just bare out of West Point, is goin' to tell me where I ride, by God!"

He'd whipped a new spark of life in Ed Harvey with the stimulant of anger, Quarterhill knew as he went forward along the column once more. But Ed Harvey was only one. Tiredness and discouragement ran even more strongly in the others, and he had no easy remedy for that. Except to drive —drive them as he was driving himself. His mouth flattened out as he clumped on through the mud. Well, then he'd drive, by God!

Ex-Corporal Clendenning, skulking at the tail of the column, had heard the words that had passed between Quarterhill and Harvey. He was sitting with his back against a tree and the misery of wet clothes, chafing him unmercifully as he moved, fed the dark anger that ran in him. He had involuntarily reached for his carbine at the sound of Quarterhill's voice in the darkness—then had relaxed again. His hate for Quarterhill had become a consuming mania now, but his native cunning told him that he had better wait. This was not the time or the place, he decided. Tomorrow, when they met Hat, would be the time.

He'd take a leaf out of his old pappy's book. A shot from the brush . . . and who could prove that it wasn't a Sioux bullet that got Quarterhill? That was the way it would be. With the last of his whiskey gone, he could expect no help from Faro now, Clendenning knew. It didn't matter. He wanted the personal satisfaction of settling the score with Webb Quarterhill; he hadn't forgotten the feel of those blows across the face or the way that he'd been shamed in front of the men he had bullied.

He heard Quarterhill's final words, listened to the sound of the other man's steps dying away in the clammy darkness. He swore violently under his breath as the collar of his shirt chafed his raw neck once more. Then he grinned

147

wolfishly with thick lips; he would be staying close to Quarterhill tomorrow!

It was after midnight and the clouds were beginning to break when word came up the column to Quarterhill that the wagon had smashed a wheel and would have to be abandoned. They were close to the headwaters of the Fourth of July now; two halts back, Mitch Garbish and his point had led the march away from the creek and onto the spine of a long ridge, rough as a devil's den, which climbed toward the divide where Ghost Basin should be. Rocky outcrops, sheer as small cliffs, had to be skirted across treacherous rock slides, and it was on one of these that the wagon had come to grief. Nobody's fault—just something that happened.

A faint starlight lay across the ridge as Quarterhill came to the spot where Dolliver and his squad worked with Amen Jones. They had carried Lieutenant Miller to the far side of the slide and put him down where the ridge flattened out a little. Quarterhill dropped on one knee beside the wounded officer and sensed, rather than saw, that Miller's eyes were open and watching him.

"Quarterhill?" Miller's voice was weak, but full awareness was in it. "What time is it?"

"After midnight. How are you doing, lieutenant?"

"Leave me here and go on," Miller said. "After you've settled with Hat . . . you can send back for me."

"We'll rig a mule litter," Quarterhill told him roughly as he got to his feet. "Nobody stays behind."

"That's an . . . order . . . Quarterhill. . . ."

For a moment Quarterhill stood looking down, his face sober and thoughtful in the starlight. What Jacob Miller said made sense; Miller was a soldier and he knew the added burden that a wounded man put on Q Troop, whose chances were thin enough at best. Yet the troop would fight the better tomorrow for the knowledge that Webb Quarterhill had left none of his wounded behind. It was as simple as that.

"Sorry, lieutenant," he answered gently. "You forget that I am giving the orders now. Just take it easy. The troop will reach the basin in time."

He moved on, passing two troopers who had led the

148

mules across the slide; the starlight showed him the vague shape of the crippled wagon as he came to where Dolliver stood, looking down helplessly. Amen Jones and a slight trooper whom Quarterhill didn't recognize immediately knelt beside Ladue. Quarterhill sank to his heels, pushing the small trooper aside.

"Give me room, soldier," he said, his voice harsh as he heard the dry *râle* of Ladue's breathing. "It's Quarterhill, Frenchy. Just take it easy. We'll rig a litter. . . ."

"No good, Reb," Ladue answered in a whisper so low that Quarterhill barely heard. "I've had it. . . . It's all right. . . . Where's Amen? . . . I'd like it if he'd say a word for me. . . . Maybe it's a good thing . . . for a man to have a word said. . . ."

"Sure, I'll do that, Frenchy," Amen Jones said, his voice a little husky. "Is there a special word you'd like?"

"That one you said back at Jensen's. . . . That was good. . . . I'd like the same one . . . Amen . . ."

For the second time in two days Amen Jones spoke the words from the Gospel of St. Luke, reciting from memory now. ". . . *for they are equal unto the angels, and they are the children of God, being the children of the resurrection.* . . ."

A small quiet lay over the little group in the starlight as Jones murmured softly, "In Thy name . . . amen."

Then Ladue's faint whisper came again. "Thanks, friend . . . You're a good little man. . . ." he said and died. Beside Quarterhill, the small trooper made a choked sound, head bent, and Quarterhill saw that it was Lee Howell, dressed in trousers and jacket that were Jacob Miller's. He got tiredly to his feet once more.

"Take him to the ridge," he said to Dolliver in a toneless voice. "We'll be moving on."

They pushed on by him, leaving him alone with Lee. Quarterhill felt a remote tug of tenderness run in him as he looked down at her. She seemed strangely boyish in the uniform that was too large for her. She stood looking up at him, the faint starlight showing her eyes large and dark against the pale oval of her face. The two didn't speak for a moment.

"We will be nearing the Basin soon, captain," Lee said

149

then in level tones. "You will need a guide. I have been up here with my father before; I had better accompany you. There is nothing more that I can do for Lieutenant Miller now."

Quarterhill nodded soberly. "Perhaps that will be best, Lee," he told her, using her given name without awkwardness. He added slowly, "I think that Ladue died easier because you were here. I am grateful for that."

The ridge joined another that climbed at a more gentle grade toward the northwest now. Tiredness was a leaden poison that ran in Quarterhill as he plodded up, towing his dead-beat mount after him. Lee Howell moved at his side. She marched with a man's easy stride; she would be a wife that a soldier could take pride in, Quarterhill thought dully. Then he put that thought away. It was dangerous ground on which he dare not tread.

He held up his hand and called out a hoarse order, and the column ground to one of its innumerable halts. This time Quarterhill didn't go back but braced himself against a ledge while Lee sat beside him. At first they didn't talk, content to enjoy the luxury of not moving for a little while. Ahead, he could see where a third ridge came in to form a rough U, vaguely discernible in the uncertain light. He looked at his watch. It was quarter past three; a little more than two hours remained before daylight. Too little time.

He asked then, "That is the Basin ahead?"

"Yes," Lee told him.

"How far, do you think?"

"Perhaps an hour's march if you go straight in," Lee said quietly. "You will not go that way?"

Quarterhill shook his head. "Hat will be expecting us to do that. We'll swing to the west—come in from there."

"Then you are going to have to push your men hard, captain," Lee said, looking up at him gravely. "There is a pass that enters the basin from the west, but it will be a race to reach there by daylight, I'm afraid."

"Then we'll race," Quarterhill said grimly.

"You'll not try to treat with Hat?"

"After Jensen's—his attack on us yesterday? It would be

150

useless. No, I hope to surprise him—hit him with all of the punch we have left. Scatter the council he's gathering."

The silence fell between them once more, each conscious that time was running out. Quarterhill was mustering his will to shove himself erect and give the command to march again when Lee spoke, her voice soft and troubled.

"And after Hat, what happens, Webb?"

Quarterhill knew what she meant and deliberately chose to disregard it. "We'll start back for McKeogh," he said evenly. "You said that Colonel Bexar had ordered reinforcements to come by train. It is my hope that they will arrive in time to complete the mopping up for us."

"That was not my question, Webb," Lee said soberly. "What about you? What will you do?"

"Go back to being Recruit Quarterhill," Webb said, more harshly than he had intended. "What else?"

"Have you forgotten Mark Faro? *He* will not have forgotten that you struck him. You superseded him in command. He will not forgive either of those things."

"No, he will not forgive that," Quarterhill murmured. "It changes nothing. It is time to go on."

Lee placed a hand on his arm, delaying him for a moment longer. "No matter what happens today, I want you to know something, Webb Quarterhill," she said. "I kissed you last night before we marched. Will you kiss me now?"

Quarterhill looked at her in the starlight; then he took her face between his hands and kissed her on the mouth—felt his kiss returned. It was a long moment that held a wild sweetness for both of them. He released her and straightened, moving away a little, and Lee was smiling with a quiet sureness.

"Now everything is all right," she said.

Day was close at hand in Ghost Basin.

15

A Trumpet in the Morning

Provisional Q Troop, stumbling dead-beat from its long swing to the west, came finally to the timber as day was beginning to break. It dropped tiredly in its tracks as Quarterhill, taking Garbish, Ed Harvey, and Dolliver with him, went forward through the scattered timber for a look. Here was a high meadow, perhaps a mile across, Quarterhill estimated as they lay under cover at the edge of the trees. Early mist hung above the small stream that wound between grassy banks in the center of the Basin. It was one of the small feeders of Loon Creek, which headed up here to flow down the far side of the divide, Quarterhill guessed.

On the near side of the stream, Sioux lodges made tall cones in the graying light; apparently the occupants still slept, unwarned by the bypassed sentries who were watching the lower pass. To the left, a series of low hills lifted above the stream on the flank of the sleeping camp, and beyond these, the Indian pony herd, upwind from where Q Troop lay, grazed unalarmed.

Garbish grunted, the early-morning sourness in his throat. "Thirty—forty lodges," he said. "Even allowin' for the papooses an' squaws, that could mean that Hat's got close to a hundred braves with him. That's a hell of a lot."

Quarterhill nodded without replying, his mind already slipping into familiar grooves as he made his plan. He'd put Dolliver and his squad on the nearest of those low hills; they'd take up a dismounted position and form a base of fire that would cover Q Troop's main advance. Garbish and his detail would make a wider swing and stampede the pony herd, driving it down the far side of the creek to pull Hat's braves into the open and away from the women and children in the lodges.

While Mitch and Dolliver were getting into position, he'd take the rest of the troop south through the timber to where the creek, bending sharply to the east, offered a natural flanking position. He'd hold Q there, hidden by the willows, until the right moment came; then he'd slam his horsemen in with the shock and fury of a mounted charge. He gave Garbish and Dolliver their orders, speaking with clipped words.

"Run the pony herd off to the east away from the lodges," he told Garbish. "You'll start the ball. It is my guess that the greater part of Hat's braves will be sucked across the creek; an Indian hates to fight without his horse. Dolliver, you hold your fire until the bulk of the Sioux have crossed. Then hold them there until I come with the rest of Q."

"The first dance to me," Mitch Garbish murmured with a little of his old lightheartedness. "Move out now?"

"Now," Quarterhill said tightly. "And good luck."

Garbish's grin showed for a fleeting moment. "I've served under worse captains," he said. "So long, Reb."

He and Dolliver started back through the timber as Ed Harvey allowed his breath to run out slowly. "Mitch ain't goin' to see the sunset of this day, an' he knows it," Harvey said. "It is too bad that such should be so."

"Let that go, Ed," Quarterhill said sharply. "You will take two men and stay with the lieutenant and Miss Howell." He saw the angry protest forming in Harvey's eyes and cut it short. "If anything should go wrong this morning—and it well may—get the two of them back into the hills and lie low. It is my guess that help will be coming before too long."

He didn't wait for Harvey's answer but wheeled and started back for the spot where the rest of the troop waited. The battered Mulroney, his back against a tree, watched Quarterhill come; his eyes, beneath their hairless brows, held a bright satisfaction as he spoke to the man beside him.

"Ah," he murmured in his rasping, husky voice, "a great fighter I could have made of that one if I had him in time. He is my style, bucko."

The other man grunted. "What the hell?" he asked.

"Ain't you mad at him for the beatin' he give you, Mulroney?"

"It was a good fight," Mulroney said. "Now, why should I be mad? Give me one good reason, bucko."

The mists were beginning to burn away in the Basin as Quarterhill ran his eye along the line of Q Troop as it waited, screened by willows, a quarter of a mile from the south flank of the Sioux camp. Thirty-one men, Quarterhill was thinking. Thirty-one tired, dirty, and worn men mounted on horses as jaded as they. Yet he felt content. There was something in the way that Q Troop sat in its saddles that spelled out "soldier," and he knew that this was a good outfit now—not the same rabble that had dogged it back at the crossing of the Sleepy Wind.

Ed Harvey, with two men, waited a little apart at one side, Lee Howell in the lieutenant's uniform that was too large for her standing with them. As Quarterhill looked, Lee lifted her hand in a swift gesture, and he gave her a grave salute before he swung his horse and pushed through the willows to where he could see the long, flat sweep of the Basin beyond. Trooper Riviera ranged up beside him, trumpet in hand.

"When I give the word," Quarterhill said to the trumpeter, "pull the Charge out of that horn of yours like it's never been pulled before. Think you can do that, son?"

Riviera answered that with his cheerful grin. "Cap'n," he said, "when I start to blow, the devil himself will come hustlin' out of his cave to run with us."

Another horse pushed up through the screen of willows and Quarterhill dropped a hand to the butt of the gun at his hip as he saw that it was Mark Faro. He stayed his hand then as he saw Faro's face; there was a wild craziness in the man's eyes, but his voice was controlled as he spoke.

"I will ride with you, Quarterhill," he said.

"As you wish."

Quarterhill thought that there was a little mockery at the back of Faro's eyes now as he pushed his horse close. "I have done many things in my life, Quarterhill," he said. "I regret none of them. Do you understand? I regret none of them. If I had them to do over, I would do them the same."

"That is your privilege, major," Quarterhill said curtly. "Do not expect me to care."

The mockery suddenly left Faro's eyes now. He said, as if he spoke to himself, "Perhaps many things will be settled this morning. I do not know." He let the thought hang there as he turned his horse back into the brush.

Quarterhill had no time to guess what lay behind the man's words because the sound of a carbine made a *spang* far across the valley now; more shots made a ragged volley in the early morning. Quarterhill straightened in the saddle, watching from where the willows screened him. The faint yells of Garbish and his men were suddenly swallowed by the rumble of pounding hoofs as the pony herd stampeded into a wild run.

The first of the sun was just touching the mountains to the east and mist still hung in the Basin, imparting an eerie unreality to the scene that was unfolding in front of Quarterhill. The Sioux camp exploded into frenzied activity as half-naked braves poured out of the lodges, weapons in hand. A few were mounted, and they made frantic efforts to head the pony herd, and succeeded in diverting a part of it to mill crazily as dust boiled up now to turn the mist into a yellow haze.

Quarterhill swore under his breath as he saw that more and more braves were getting mounted now. He damned Dolliver for waiting too long to open up, let his breath go out as he saw little puffs, made by black powder, blossom against the low hillside to the left. After a moment the solid sound of the carbines reached his ears. The flanking fire put fresh confusion into the wheeling riders out in front, and it was time to go.

He swung his arm up, calling over his shoulder, "Forward . . . walk . . . hoooo!" then swung his arm forward and down as he spurred out of the willows.

They left the shelter of the trees, dressing their line, and Quarterhill quickened the gait to a trot. The mass of the Sioux were a quarter mile ahead, and he headed the troop into the center of them, holding down the pace until they had covered half the distance. It was time now to make his move, Quarterhill knew.

He sang out, "Gallop . . . hoooo!" A moment later he

155

flung "Sound the charge!" at Riviera, and lifted a last effort out of his tired mount, putting it into a run.

He heard the solid pound of hoofs behind him, and he turned a little in his saddle to look back. What he saw filled him with a fierce exultation. Provisional Q Troop had found itself. It was coming on, its line as steady as if on parade; troopers bent low over saddlebows, pistols held high in right hands and reins held low in left. A good troop!

Quarterhill turned back, and a moment later he was among the Sioux. First the fringe of dismounted men, scattering before the fury of the charge, then a solid phalanx of horsemen, and the fight boiled up in bell-toned hurrah as rider crashed into rider. The Basin exploded into a wild melee of wheeling horses and yelling men, the whole punctuated by the crack of gunfire.

A dismounted brave tried to gut Quarterhill's horse with a lance, went down tumbling as Quarterhill's bullet caught him in the chest. He spurred on toward a squat, ugly man wearing a streaming war bonnet. Hat, he guessed. Now Mulroney ranged alongside him, yelling barroom curses with a lusty elation.

"Hit 'em in the belly, bucko! That's the style!"

Fire came from the left in increasing volume, and Quarterhill saw Mulroney's horse stumble, Mulroney going over its head in a long fall. No time to think of that now. Hat was ahead, rallying his warriors, and Quarterhill, with half a dozen men of Q Troop behind him, smashed into the milling group.

A horse screamed with a high keen of sound; more riders were going down into the boil of the dust. An arrow struck Quarterhill's horse in the neck, turning it crazy with fear and pain. As he fought to bring the animal back under control, Quarterhill saw Hat pushing his pony forward, a knobbed war club swung high above his head. A blue-clad horseman flashed by, and Quarterhill saw that it was Mark Faro. The dark cynicism had gone out of the major's face now, leaving it serene—almost happy—as Faro's mount bolted into Hat's pony.

The rising sun glinted on the war club as it crashed down and Faro left his saddle, dead before he hit the ground. But Faro had given Quarterhill the tiny fraction of a second that he needed. *You have paid your bill in full, Mark Faro,* he thought as he laid the sights of his revolver full on Hat's painted chest dead ahead of him now. He squeezed the trigger and felt the hard jump of the gun against the crotch of his hand—heard Hat's choked death cry as he went over backward into the rising dust.

Quarterhill thought: *And that pays another bill. It pays in part for what was done at Jensen's, God damn you!*

The blow that slammed into Webb Quarterhill's back came a split instant before he heard the crack of the carbine behind him. It sounded loud and very clear. In the last second before darkness came to engulf him he thought with a deep resignation: *One of Q's troopers fired that shot. . . . It is too bad . . . yet it solves many things . . . many things . . .*

Trooper Mulroney lay where he had fallen, all feeling gone from his legs and a dreamy peacefulness beginning to creep over him. He'd been mortally hurt, he knew. He lay at the edge of a clump of brush a little above the creek's bed, and like a picture seen through a hazy glass, he watched the fight swirl on ahead of him. *A grand fight,* he thought. Then he said aloud, "You wouldn't have missed it, bucko. You wouldn't have missed it. . . ."

The few Sioux who were still mounted were drawing off toward the hills to the east now. Farther up the creek, Dolliver's dismounted men were rounding up the squaws and children among the lodges. Mulroney saw Hat go down beneath Quarterhill's bullet. Then he was dimly aware that he was not alone here by the creek bank. With an effort he lifted his head to see better.

A man was creeping through the brush on hands and knees, and Mulroney recognized Clendenning now. He watched, bemused, as the thick-set ex-corporal crouched and brought his carbine to his shoulder. Too late, Mulroney understood as the gun went *spang*. He saw the wisp of blue smoke drift up from the muzzle; then he turned his head in time to see Quarterhill slump from the saddle fifty yards away. A faint sadness stirred Mulroney then.

His own weapon was lying a yard from his hand, where it

had fallen when he had gone down. With a vast and terrible effort, he inched himself toward the gun. He got his fingers around the grip and lifted it, steadying it with both hands as he lay there. He must be slow and careful, he knew, because the feeling was going out of his arms and fingers now. With the jerky movements of a puppet he pulled the hammer back—saw Clendenning's head swivel around with a startled jerk and comprehension come into the other's eyes as the sights steadied against his thick shoulders.

Fear held the ex-corporal frozen for long enough. His mouth made a round O as he called hoarsely, "No! Don't do it, Mulroney!"

"Ah, bucko," Mulroney murmured, "I said that I would pull a trigger at your execution," and he squeezed his forefinger tight with the last of the will that was left in him.

With satisfaction, he saw Clendenning's heavy body jerk, then lie still. The gun dropped into the dirt and Mulroney's battered face was satisfied as he cradled it in his arms.

"A good fight . . ." he said.

Mitch Garbish and his five men had been half a mile away up the meadow when Q Troop's charge had gone in; Garbish had swung his few men and led them on from the flank, pushing the tired horses to the last of their endurance. They were abreast of the first of the lodges when Garbish, a dozen yards ahead of the rest, saw Quarterhill slide limply out of his saddle and go head first down into the dirt. A solid fury gripped the big man as he whirled his horse and started at a run in that direction.

One of the last of the mounted Sioux, yelling crazily, flashed by, firing as he passed, and Garbish felt his ribs smash beneath the impact of the bullet. He swayed in the saddle but went on, his anger sustaining him, dismounted then, and somehow got the unconscious Quarterhill across his own saddle.

He was moving slowly back toward the willows when he saw Ed Harvey coming on. Now the tiredness suddenly took possession of Mitch Garbish and he stopped and waited, clinging to his horse's mane to keep from falling. Harvey saw the dark, spreading stain on Garbish's shirt, dismounted hastily, and slid an arm about the other to keep him from toppling into the dirt.

"Ease down, Mitch," Harvey said hoarsely. "You're hit bad, man. Let me have a look!"

Garbish shook his head, still holding himself erect. "See to Quarterhill, Ed," he whispered, using a vast effort to force the words out as the old good humor came back into his face for a brief moment. "He is too good a man to lose . . . even for a Rebel. Ah, well . . . have had my fun. I told you that my luck had run out. . . ." Now his knees buckled beneath him and he fell forward, his face in the dew-wet grass.

It was dark again when Quarterhill came back from the far trails where he had been riding. All at once his perceptions were very acute, and he wondered idly if that could be because he was dying. He had heard that dying could be like that. He didn't care very much.

He could smell the pungent spice of pine and sage. There were stars over his head, and they seemed very bright and very close. Wind fanned his face a little—cool and good—and went on to make its gentle rustling sounds through the trees. The whisper of angel's wings, Quarterhill thought and wondered where he had heard that before. Not that it mattered . . .

Pain came then—a long, searing flame of it that grabbed him in its vise so that he bit on a lip to keep from crying out. It burned like a malignant bonfire in his chest, putting icy sweat on his forehead. Then he was aware that shadowy figures were moving around him in the dark, and a voice that he didn't recognize said bluffly, "Get a little of this into your belly, my friend. He felt his head being lifted as a bottle touched his lips.

The voice spoke again. "He'll do for now. The man's got the constitution of an ox, Miss Howell. When daylight comes I'll have that bullet out of him, and barring a few minor mishaps like gangrene or pneumonia, he'll be fit as a fiddle again in practically no time at all."

The whiskey was driving the pain farther back in Quarterhill now—replacing it with a comforting warmth. The shapes around him were moving away. A gentle hand touched the stubble on his cheek and he caught a faint hint of that perfume that had crowded his dreams, so that he knew Lee Howell was kneeling beside him now. He was content to lie, not talking, for a moment longer while he soaked in the comfort of her presence.

She murmured then, "Everything is going to be all right, darling. Everything is going to be fine."

"Yes," he said slowly, wanting to hang onto this as long as he could. "Who was that who was here?"

"Dr. Nolan," Lee answered. "Colonel Bexar sent help. . . . They got here last night. The troop did not need them, but they brought a doctor. So everything will be all right."

Quarterhill didn't hear the last words because that quick surge of pride had run through him again at the mention of Q Troop. "No, Q Troop didn't need them," he said softly, savoring the words. "It is a good troop. . . . I would be proud to command it again. . . . That is not possible, of course. . . ."

Lee's fingers touched his lips and she said, "Don't try to talk now, Webb. You may have a command sooner than you think. Lieutenant Miller is going to recover; he told Dr. Nolan that he was damned if he was going to die before he had seen you in the uniform of an officer of the United States Army, where you belong. He means that. I know that Colonel Bexar will back him up."

For a moment Quarterhill thought of that; then he accepted it with the quiet happiness of a man who has been long away but who has at last come home. A drowsy content began to flow in him as he found Lee's hand and pulled her close. He slept, then, with the memory of her lips on his own.